Treasures of the Snow

Patricia St John

Revised by Mary Mills

Illustrated by Gary Rees

MOODY PUBLISHERS
CHICAGO

Interior and Cover Design: Ragont Design
Cover Illustration: Matthew Archambault

ISBN-13: 978-0-8024-6575-7
Printed by Color House Graphics in Grand Rapids, MI–07/2016

We hope you enjoy this book from Moody Publishers. Our goal is to provide high-quality, thought-provoking books and products that connect truth to your real needs and challenges. For more information on other books and products written and produced from a biblical perspective, go to www.moodypublishers.com or write to:

Moody Publishers
820 N. LaSalle Boulevard
Chicago, IL 60610

15 17 19 20 18 16 14

Printed in the United States of America

Contents

Revised Edition

It has been over fifty years since the first editions of Patricia St. John's *Treasures of the Snow* and *The Tanglewoods' Secret* were published, and they have become classics of their time.

In these new editions, Mary Mills has sensitively adapted the language of the books for a new generation of children, while preserving Patricia St. John's superb skill as a storyteller.

A note from the author

When I was a child of seven I went to live in Switzerland. My home was a chalet on the mountain, above the village where I have imagined Annette and Dani to live.

Like them, I went to the village school on a sled by moonlight, and helped to make hay in summer. I followed the cows up the mountain, and slept in the hay. I went to church on Christmas Eve to see the tree covered with oranges and gingerbread bears, and was taken to visit the doctor in the town up the valley. Klaus was my own white kitten, given to me by a farmer, and my baby brothers rode in the milk cart behind the great St. Bernard dog.

But all this was over twenty years ago, and I have

been back only as a visitor; Switzerland today is probably very different. I expect it would be impossible now for a child to miss school for any length of time, and no doubt the medical service has improved. Perhaps all little villages have their own doctors now. I do not know.

But I do know that today, as twenty years ago, the little school and the church still stand, the cowbells still tinkle in the valley, and the narcissi still scent the fields in May. And I hope that little children still sing carols under the tree at Christmas and love their gingerbread bears as much as I loved mine.

I have not given the village its proper name, because for the sake of the story, I have added one or two things that are not really there. For instance, there is no town nearby that could not be reached except by the Pass. But otherwise I have tried to keep it true to life, and if ever you go to Switzerland and take an electric train up from Montreux you will stop at a tiny station where hayfields bound the platform and high green hills rise up behind, dotted with chalets. To the right of the railway the banks drop down into a foaming, rushing river, beyond which the mountains rise again, and between a long, green mountain and a rocky, pointed mountain there lies a Pass. If, added to all this, you see a low white school building not far from the station and a wooden church spire rising from behind a hillock, you will know that this is the village where this story was born.

Patricia St. John
1950

1

Christmas Eve

It was Christmas Eve, and three people were climbing the steep, white mountainside, the moonlight throwing shadows behind them across the snow. The middle one was a woman in a long skirt with a dark cloak over her shoulders. Clinging to her hand was a black-haired boy of six, who talked all the time with his mouth full. Walking a little way away from them, with her eyes turned to the stars, was a girl of seven. Her hands were folded across her chest, and close to her heart she carried a golden gingerbread bear with eyes made of white icing.

The little boy had also had a gingerbread bear, but he had eaten it all except the back legs. He looked at the girl spitefully. "Mine was bigger than yours," he said.

The girl did not seem upset. "I would not change it," she replied calmly, without turning her head. Then she looked down again with eyes full of love at the beautiful bear in her arms. How solid he looked, how delicious he smelled, and how brightly he gleamed in the starlight. She would never eat him, never!

Eighty little village children had been given gingerbread bears, but hers had surely been by far the most beautiful.

Yes, she would keep him forever in memory of tonight, and whenever she looked at him she would remember Christmas Eve—the frosty blue sky, the warm glow of the lighted church, the tree decorated with silver stars, the carols, the crib, and the sweet, sad story of Christmas. It made her want to cry when she thought about the inn where there was no room. She would have opened her door wide and welcomed Mary and Joseph in.

Lucien, the boy, was annoyed by her silence. "I have nearly finished mine," he remarked, scowling. "Let me taste yours, Annette. You have not started it." But Annette shook her head and held her bear a little closer. "I am never going to eat him," she replied. "I am going to keep him forever and ever."

They had come to where the crumbly white path divided. A few hundred yards along the right fork stood a group of chalets with lights shining in their windows and dark barns standing behind them. Annette was nearly home.

Madame Morel hesitated. "Are you all right to run home alone, Annette?" she asked doubtfully, "or shall we take you to the door?"

"Oh, I would much rather go home alone," answered Annette, "and thank you for taking me. Good night, Madame; good night, Lucien."

She turned and ran, in case Madame should change her mind and insist on seeing her to the door. She so badly wanted to be alone.

She wanted to get away from Lucien's chatter and enjoy the silence of the night. How could she think, and look at the stars, when she was having to make polite replies to Madame Morel and Lucien?

She had never been out alone at night before, and even this was a sort of accident. She was supposed to have gone to the church on the sleigh with her parents. They had all been thinking about it and planning it for weeks. But that morning her mother had been taken ill and her father had gone off on the midday train to fetch the doctor from the town up the valley. The doctor had arrived about teatime, but he could not cure her in time to get up and go to church as Annette had hoped he would, so to her great disappointment she had to go instead with Madame Morel from the chalet up the hill. But when she had reached the church it had been so beautiful that she had forgotten everything but the tree and the magic of Christmas, so it had not mattered so much after all.

The magic stayed with her, and now, as she stood alone among snow and stars, it seemed a pity to go in just yet and break the spell. She hesitated as she reached the steps leading up to the balcony and looked around. Just opposite loomed the cowshed;

Annette could hear the beasts moving and munching from the manger.

An exciting idea struck her. She made up her mind in a moment, darted across the sleigh tracks, and lifted the latch of the door. The warm smell of cattle and milk and hay greeted her as she slipped inside. She wriggled against the legs of the chestnut-colored cow and wormed her way into the hayrack. The cow was having supper, but Annette flung her arms around its neck and let it go on munching, just as the cows must have munched when Mary sat among them with her newborn baby in her arms.

She looked down at the manger and imagined Baby Jesus was lying in the straw with the cows, still and quiet, worshipping about Him. Through a hole in the roof she could see one bright star, and she remembered how a star had shone over Bethlehem and guided the wise men to the house where Jesus lay. She could imagine them padding up the valley on their swaying camels. And surely any moment now the door would open softly and the shepherds would come creeping in with little lambs in their arms and offer to cover the child with woolly fleeces. As she leaned further, a great feeling of pity came over her for the homeless baby who had had all the doors shut against him.

"There would have been plenty of room in our chalet," she whispered, "and yet perhaps after all this is the nicest place. The hay is sweet and clean and Louise's breath is warm and pleasant. Maybe God chose the best cradle for his baby after all."

She might have stayed there dreaming all night if it

had not been for the gleam of a lantern through the half-open door of the shed and the sound of firm, crunchy footsteps in the snow.

Then she heard her father call her in a quick, hurried voice.

She slipped down from the rack, dodged Louise's tail, and ran out to him with wide-open arms.

"I went in to wish the cows a happy Christmas," she said, laughing. "Did you come out to find me?"

"Yes, I did," he replied, but he was not laughing. His face was pale and serious in the moonlight, and he took her hand and almost dragged her up the steps. "You should have come in at once, with your mother so ill. She has been asking for you for half an hour."

Annette suddenly felt very sorry, for somehow the Christmas tree had made her forget about everything else, and all the time her mother, whom she loved so much, was lying ill and wanting her. She had thought the doctor would have made her better. She took her hand out from her father's and ran up the wooden stairs and into her mother's bedroom.

Neither the doctor nor the village nurse saw her until she had crept up to the bed, for she was a small, slim child who moved almost silently. But her mother saw her and half held out her arms. Annette, without a word, ran into them and hid her face on her mother's shoulder. She began to cry quietly, for her mother's face was almost as white as the pillow and it frightened her. Besides, she felt sorry for having been away so long.

"Annette," whispered her mother, "stop crying. I

have a present for you."

Annette stopped at once. A present? Of course, it was Christmas. She had quite forgotten. Her mother always gave her a present, but she usually had it on New Year's Day. Wherever could it be? She looked around expectantly.

Her mother turned to the nurse. "Give it to her," she whispered. The nurse pulled back the blanket and lifted out a bundle wrapped in a white shawl. She came around to Annette and held it out to her.

"Your little brother," the nurse explained. "Let us go down by the fire and you shall rock his cradle. We must leave your mother to sleep. Kiss her good night."

"Your little brother," echoed her mother's weak voice. "He is yours, Annette. Bring him up and love him and look after him for me. I give him to you."

Her voice trailed away and she closed her eyes. Annette, too dazed to speak, allowed herself to be led downstairs by the nurse. She sat down on a stool by the stove to rock the wooden cradle where her Christmas present lay covered in shawls and blankets.

She sat very still for a long time staring at the bump that was her little brother. The house was very still, and the Christmas star shone in through the windows as it had shone on that other Christmas baby in the stable at Bethlehem, with Mary sitting watching God's little Son, just as she was sitting by the stove watching her little brother.

She put out gentle fingers and touched the top of his downy head, which was all she could see of him.

Then with a tired sigh she leaned her head against the cradle and let her imagination go where it would—stars, shepherds, little new babies, shut doors, wise men, and gingerbread bears—they all became muddled up in her mind, and she slid gradually onto the floor.

It was here that her father found her an hour later, lying as peacefully asleep as her new baby brother, her bright head resting on the cradle rocker.

"Poor little motherless creatures," he said as he stooped to pick her up. "How shall I ever bring them up without her?"

For Annette's mother had gone to spend Christmas in heaven.

2

Grandmother Arrives

So Daniel Burnier, age three hours, became the special property of Annette Burnier, age seven years.

Of course, the kind village nurse stayed for some time to bathe and feed him, and when she left, her father paid a woman from the village to come and nurse him. But Dani belonged to Annette, and nobody ever spoke of him as anything but Annette's baby.

For once the first great shock of losing her mother was over, Annette gathered up all the love of her sad, lonely little heart and poured it out on her little brother. She held his bottle while he sucked and sat quietly by his cradle in case he should wake and want her. It was Annette who ran to him in the night if he woke or whimpered, and who carried him out onto the balcony at midday so that the sun might shine on him. And with so much love and sunshine surrounding him, the baby grew strong, until there was no other baby of his age in the valley who was as healthy and beautiful. He slept and woke and chuckled and fed and kicked and slept again. In fact, he never gave a moment's worry to anyone.

"He was born under a lucky star," exclaimed a woman from the village, gazing at him thoughtfully.

"He was born under a Christmas star," said Annette solemnly. "I think he will always be good and happy."

And how he grew! By the time the sun was beginning to melt the snow, and the crocuses were pushing up in the pale fields, Annette was having to think about new clothes. As soon as the cows had gone up the mountain, Dani cut his first tooth. As Annette knew nothing about first teeth, and expected no trouble, the baby himself forgot that it should have been a painful time, so instead of fretting and crying he just giggled and sucked his fists.

Soon Dani was moving around, and his cradle could hold him no longer. He wanted to explore everything from the stove to the balcony steps, and Annette spent an anxious few weeks keeping him out of danger. In the end she decided to tie him by one pink foot to the leg of the kitchen table and he explored in circles, and life became more peaceful.

It was just about this time that Annette, slipping down to the living room after tucking Dani up in his cradle, found her father sitting by the stove with his head in his hands, looking old and tired and grey. He had often looked old and tired since his wife died, but tonight he looked worse than usual. Annette, who tried hard to make up for her mother, climbed onto his knee and laid her soft cheek against his bony brown one.

"What is the matter, Papa?" she asked. "Are you very tired tonight? Shall I make you a cup of coffee?"

He looked down at her curiously for a minute or two. She was so small and light, like a golden-haired fairy, but how sensible and womanly she was! Somehow during the past year he had made a habit of telling her his troubles and even listening to her serious advice. So now he pulled her head against his shoulder and told her all about it.

"We shall have to sell some of the cows, little daughter," he explained sadly. "We must have some more money or there will be no winter boots for you."

Annette lifted her head and stared at him in horror. They only had ten cows, and each one was a personal friend. Any one of them would be missed terribly. She must think of a better way to earn money than that.

"You see," her father went on, "other men have wives to look after their little ones. I have to pay a woman to nurse Dani, and it is expensive. Yet someone must look after him, poor little lad."

Annette sat up very straight and tossed back her plaits. She knew exactly what to do, and all she had to do was make her father agree.

"Papa," she said very slowly and distinctly, "you

do not need Mademoiselle Mottier any longer. I am eight and a half now, and I can look after Dani as well as anyone. You will not have to pay me anything, and then we can keep the cows. Why, think, Papa, how unhappy they would be to leave us! I do believe Paquerette would cry!"

"But you must go to school," said her father rather doubtfully. "It would not be right to keep you at home, and anyhow it is against the law. The schoolmaster would want to know why, and he would tell the mayor and we should get into trouble."

"But it is much more important to look after Dani," answered Annette, wrinkling her forehead, "and if you explained to the master, he would understand. He is a kind man, and he is a friend of yours. Let's try it and see what happens. I will do my lessons here in the kitchen, Papa, every morning, and Dani can play on the floor. In any case, it's only for four years. When Dani is five he will go to the infant school, and I can take him down and go to the big school."

Her father continued to look at her thoughtfully. Although she was small, she was as clever as a woman in looking after the baby, and she was very handy about the house. But she could not do the cooking, or knit the stockings, or do the rough heavy work. And besides, she ought to have some schooling. He sat thinking in silence for a full five minutes. Then *he* had an idea.

"I wonder if your grandmother would come," he said suddenly. "She is old and has rheumatics, and her sight is poor, but she could do the cooking and mending perhaps, and she could help you with your lessons in the evenings. It would be company for you, too, when I am up the mountain. You're a little girl to be left alone all day long. If I write a letter to the schoolmaster telling him that Grandmother will give you a bit of teaching, maybe he will agree to keep quiet about it."

Annette climbed off his knee, and fetched two sheets of paper and a pen and ink from the cupboard.

"Write to them both now," she said, "and I will post them when I go for the bread. Then we shall get the answers nice and quickly."

Both letters were answered that week. The first answer was Grandmother herself, who arrived by train, bent and crippled, with a wooden box roped up very securely. Annette went down to meet her and watched the little electric train twisting its way up the valley between the hay fields like a caterpillar. It was rather late, the driver explained angrily, because a cow had strayed onto the line and the train had had to stop. He moved off so quickly that Grandmother hardly had time to get down, and her wooden box had to be thrown out after her while the train was moving away.

Grandmother, however, did not seem at all worried. She leaned on her stick and wanted to know how she was going to get up the hill. Annette, who knew nothing about rheumatism, suggested that they should walk, but Grandmother said, "Nonsense, child," and in the end they got a lift in an empty farm cart that had brought cheeses down to the train and was now going back up the mountain.

The road was stony, the wheels wooden, and the mule uncertain, and Annette enjoyed the ride very much more than Grandmother did. But the old woman gritted her teeth and made no complaint. She only let out a tired sigh of relief when she found herself safely on the sofa by the stove, with a cushion at her aching back and Annette bustling about getting her some tea.

Dani came out from under the table, getting along on his bottom. He stuck three fingers in his mouth and laughed at Grandmother, who put on her glasses to see him better. They sat for some moments staring at each other, her dim old eyes meeting his bright blue ones, and then Dani threw back his head and laughed again.

"That child will wear out his trousers," said Grandmother, taking a piece of bread and butter and cherry jam. "He should be taught to crawl."

She said no more until she had finished her tea, and then she flicked the crumbs from her black skirt and got up, leaning heavily on her stick.

"So," she remarked, "I have come. What I can I will do; what I cannot you must do for me. Now, Annette, turn that baby the right way up and come and show me around the kitchen." And from that moment Grandmother did what she could, Annette did the rest, and the household ran like clockwork. All except for Dani, who continued to move round and round the table legs on his bottom in spite of Grandmother. So after a few days Annette was sent to the village to buy a yard of thick, black felt, and

Grandmother sewed round patches onto the seats of all Dani's trousers. He did look rather odd in them, but they served their purpose very well indeed, and after all they were hardly ever seen because they were nearly always underneath him.

The second answer arrived in the shape of the old village schoolmaster, who walked wearily up from the valley late on Saturday afternoon to call on Monsieur Burnier. He was milking cows and saw him coming out the cowshed window. He did not want to argue with the schoolmaster because he was afraid of getting the worst of it, so he ran out the back door and hid in the hayloft. Annette, who was also looking out of the living room window, saw her father's legs disappear up the ladder just as the schoolmaster came around the corner, and she understood perfectly what was expected of her.

She opened the door and invited the master in, offering him most politely the best chair with a smart red seat. He was very fond of Annette, and Annette was very fond of him, but today they were a little bit shy of each other. Grandmother folded her hands and sat up straight like an old warhorse ready for battle.

"I have come to see your father," began the school-master, coughing nervously, "to discuss his letter about you being away from school. I cannot say that I think it right for a little girl of your age. Besides, it is against the law of the State."

"The State will know nothing about it unless you choose to mention her," said Grandmother. "Besides, I will teach the child myself. I do not think it right for a little boy of Dani's age to be left without his sister to look after him."

"But can't you look after him?" suggested the schoolmaster gently.

"Certainly not," snapped Grandmother. "My sight is so poor that I cannot see where he is going, and my arms are so rheumaticky that I cannot pick him up if he falls. Besides, he moves like an express train, and I am nearly eighty. You do not know what you are talking about."

The schoolmaster gazed at Dani, who was face-downwards in the woodpile eating shavings. There was nothing much to be seen of him but the black felt patches and his dimpled brown legs. The master realized Grandmother would not be able to manage him.

The schoolmaster didn't know what to do. Perhaps his old friend Monsieur Burnier would be more reasonable. He turned to Annette. "When will your father be in, Annette?" he asked.

"I don't know. He has gone out and he may not be back for some time. It is not worth your while to wait, monsieur," replied Annette steadily, knowing perfectly well that her father would return just as soon as the master disappeared down the valley.

The schoolmaster sat thinking. He was a good man, and really cared about Annette and his duty toward her. Yet he did not want to give up his old friend into the hands of the law, especially when it was quite clear that the child was needed at home. At last he had an idea. He did not think that it was a very good one, but it was better than nothing.

"I will let the matter rest," he said at last, "on one condition only. And that is that every Saturday morning, when Annette comes down for the bread, she shall visit me in my house and I will test her. If I find she is making progress I will say no more, but if I find she is learning nothing then I shall feel it my duty to insist that she attends school like other children."

He tried to speak sternly, but Annette beamed at him, and Dani, sensing a family victory, suddenly turned himself the right way up and crowed like a cock. The schoolmaster looked at the two fair, motherless children for a moment, smiled very tenderly, and said good-bye. As soon as he had disappeared into the pine wood Annette ran to the door and called to her father to come down from the hay loft, and she told him the good news.

So it was that every Saturday morning Annette rapped at the front door of the tall, white house where the schoolmaster lived, with her bread-basket on her back and her tattered exercise book in her hand, and the schoolmaster joyfully let her in. In the winter they sat by the stove, ate spiced fruit tart, and drank hot chocolate, and in the summer they sat on the veranda and ate cherries and drank apple juice. After that the tests would begin.

They always started with arithmetic, but Annette was not good at arithmetic. As she never knew the answers, the schoolmaster would feel, after a few minutes, that it was a waste of time to ask any more questions, so they would pass on to history, and here Annette never needed any questions. She would lean forward, clasping her knees, and relate how William Tell had won the freedom of Switzerland, and how the brave little son had stood still while the apple on his head was split by the whizzing arrow. Annette knew all about the brave Swiss heroes, and she and the schoolmaster would look at each other with shining eyes, for they both loved courage. After this they would turn to the Bible, which Annette was beginning to know quite well, for she read it aloud to Grandmother every evening.

By this time the schoolmaster would have forgotten to tell Annette off because she couldn't do her sums, and instead he would give her fresh books to read and would fill the gaps in her bread basket with spiced gingerbread hearts and knobbly chocolate sticks wrapped in silver paper. Then they would say good-bye to one another, and he would stand at the door and watch her until she reached the edge of the pine wood, because here she always turned around to wave.

Years ago the schoolmaster had loved a golden-haired girl who lived high up in the mountain, and he had bought this white house and made it beautiful for her. But she went out to pick soldanellas and was killed by a treacherous fall of late snow. So the schoolmaster really lived alone. But in his dreams she was always there, and also a little daughter with corn-colored plaits and eyes like blue gentians who sat on a stool close to his knees. And on Saturday mornings that part of the school-master's dream came true.

3

A Very Special Christmas Present

It was Christmas Eve again, five years after the beginning of this story, and Dani was now five years old. It was a great day, because for the first time in his life he had been considered old enough to go down to the church with Annette and to see the tree.

He sat up in bed, drinking a bowl of potato soup, his blond hair only just showing above his enormous white feather duvet, which was almost as fat as it was wide. Annette sat beside him, and in her hand she held a shining gingerbread bear.

"I'm sorry, Dani," she said firmly, "but you cannot have it in the bed with you. It would be all crumbs by the morning. Look, I will put him here on the cupboard and the moon will shine in on him and you will be able to see him."

Dani opened his mouth to argue, but changed his mind and filled his mouth with potato soup instead. It was unfair of his sister to say he couldn't hug his bear all night, but, after all, there were lots of other things to be happy about. Dani was always happy from the moment he opened his eyes in the morning to the moment he closed them at night. Tonight he was especially happy because he had heard the bells and seen the glittering Christmas tree and been out in the snow by starlight. He handed his empty bowl to Annette and cuddled down under his feather duvet.

"Do you think," he asked, "that Father Christmas would come if I put my slippers on the window-sill?"

Annette looked rather startled and wondered where he had heard of such a thing, for in Switzerland Father Christmas is not such a well-known person as he is in England. Swiss children have their Christmas bear from the tree on Christmas Eve, and presents from their family on New Year's Day. On Christmas Day they go to church and have a feast, but few children get a present.

"They said," went on Dani, "that he came on a sleigh drawn by reindeer and left presents in good children's slippers. Am I a good child, Annette?"

"Yes," answered Annette, kissing him, "you are a very good child. But you will not get a present from Father Christmas. He only goes to rich little boys."

"Aren't I a rich little boy?" asked Dani, who thought he had everything he wanted in life.

"No," replied Annette firmly, "you are not. We are poor, and Papa has to work hard, and Grandmother and I have to go on and on patching your clothes because we cannot afford to buy new ones."

Dani chuckled. "I don't mind being poor," he said firmly. "I like it. Now tell me a story, Annette. Tell me about Christmas and the little baby and the cows and the great big shining star."

So Annette told the story, and Dani, who should have been asleep, listened with his eyes wide open.

"I should have liked sleeping in the hay better than in the inn," he said when she had finished. "I should like to sleep with Paquerette. I think it would be fun."

Annette shook her head. "No, you wouldn't," she replied, "not in the winter without a duvet. You would be very cold and unhappy and long for a warm bed. It was cruel of them to say there was no room for a little new baby—they could have made room somehow."

The cuckoo clock on the stairs struck nine. Annette jumped up.

"You must go to sleep, Dani," she said, "and I must make Papa's hot chocolate."

She kissed him, tucked him in, put out the light, and left him. But Dani did not go to sleep. Instead, he lay staring out into the darkness, thinking hard.

He was not a greedy little boy, but he could not help thinking that if Father Christmas happened to come to their house it would be a great pity not to be ready. Of course, it was unlikely he would come, since Dani was only a poor child, but on the other hand it was just possible that he might. And, after all, it wouldn't hurt to put out the little slipper even if there was nothing in it in the morning.

The question was where to put it. He could not put it on the windowsill, because he could not open the high, barred shutters by himself. Nor could he put it outside the front door, because the family was all sitting in the front room. The only place was just outside the back door on the little strip of snow that divided the kitchen from the hay barn. Of course Father Christmas probably wouldn't see it there, but still, there was no harm in trying.

Dani's mind was made up. He crept out of bed and tiptoed carefully across the bedroom and down the stairs. He went barefoot, because he did not want anyone to hear him, and in his hand he carried one small scarlet slipper lined with rabbit fur. Annette had made the slippers, and Dani felt Father Christmas might notice them as they were bright and rather unusual.

It was a struggle to lift the great wooden bar on the kitchen door, and Dani had to stand on a stool before he managed it. He had a moment's bright glimpse of snow and starlight, and then the bitter cold air struck him like a knife and almost took his breath away. He quickly pushed the slipper onto the step and shut the door again as quickly as he could.

Back to bed scuttled Dani with a light heart. He cuddled down under the bedclothes, curled himself into a ball, and buried his nose in the pillows. He had already said his proper prayers with Annette before he got into bed, but now he had a little bit to add.

"Please, dear God," he whispered, "make Father

Christmas and his reindeer come this way. And make him see my red slipper, and make him put a little present inside even if I am only a poor boy."

And then the bump that was Dani rolled over sideways and fell asleep to dream, like thousands of other children all over the world, of the old gentleman in the red cloak careening over the snow to the jangle of reindeer bells.

He woke very early, because children always wake early on Christmas morning, and of course the first thing he thought of was the scarlet slipper. It was such an exciting thought that his heart beat with great thumps, and he peeped over the top of his duvet to see whether Annette was awake.

But Annette was fast asleep, with her long, fair hair spread all over the pillow, and for all Dani knew it might still have been the middle of the night. In fact, he had almost decided that it must still be the middle of the night, when he heard his father clattering the milk churns in the kitchen below.

So it must be Christmas morning, and Dani must get down quickly or his father would open the door and find his present before he did. Somehow Dani was absolutely sure that there would be a present. All his doubts of the night before had vanished in his sleep.

He crept out of the room without waking Annette and slipped into the kitchen where his father was cleaning out the churns.

Father did not see Dani until he felt two arms clasping his legs and looked down. There was his son, rosy, bright-eyed, and with his hair all scruffy, looking up at him.

"Has Father Christmas been?" asked Dani. Surely his father, who stayed up so late and got up so early, must have heard the bells and the crunch of hoofs in the snow.

"Father Christmas?" repeated his father in a puzzled voice. "Why, no, he didn't come here. We live too far up the mountain for him."

But Dani shook his head. "We don't," he said eagerly. "His reindeer can go anywhere, and I expect you were asleep and didn't hear him. Open the door for me, Papa, in case he has left me a present."

His father wished he had known of this earlier so he could have put a chocolate stick on the step, for he hated to disappoint his boy. However, he had to open the back door to roll the churns across to the stable, so he lifted the latch. In an instant Dani had dived between his legs like an eager rabbit, and was kneeling by his slipper in the snow.

Then he gave a wild, high-pitched scream of excitement and dived back again into the kitchen with his slipper in his arms.

A miracle had happened. Father Christmas had been and had left a present, and in all his happy five years of life Dani had never had such a perfect present before.

For curled up in the furry lining of his scarlet slipper was a tiny white kitten, with blue eyes and one black smudge on her nose. It was a weak, thin little kitten, very nearly dead with cold and hunger, and if it had not been for the warmth of the rabbit fur it would certainly have been quite dead. But it still breathed lightly, and Dani's father, forgetting all about the churns, knelt down on the kitchen floor beside his son and set about making it better.

First he wrapped it in a piece of warm flannel and laid it against the hot wall of the stove. Then they heated milk in a pan and fed it with a spoon, as it was far too weak to suck. At first it only spluttered and dribbled, but after a while it put out a soft pink tongue and its dim blue eyes grew bright and interested. Then, after about five minutes or so, it twitched its tail and stretched itself. Finally, having had quite enough to eat, it curled itself back into a ball and set up a faint, contented purr.

All this time Dani and his father had not spoken one word, because they were so intent on what they were doing. But now that their work was successfully finished for the time being, they sat back and looked at each other. Dani's cheeks were the color of poppies and his eyes shone like stars.

"I knew he would come," he whispered, "but I never guessed he would bring such a beautiful present. It is the most beautiful present I have ever had in all my life. What shall I call it, Papa?"

"You had better call it Klaus after the Christmas saint," said Papa. It certainly seemed like a miracle.

Papa left the sleeping kitten in Dani's care and went to the stables. Sitting in the dim light with his head pressed against the sides of the cows and the milk frothing into the pails, he tried to think of some explanation. Of course the kitten had strayed across from the barn, but it did seem wonderful that it should have found Dani's slipper and been there all ready for him. After a while Dani's father decided that perhaps it was not so wonderful after all. Surely it was natural on Christmas night that the Father in heaven, thinking of His own Son, would not have wanted to disappoint a motherless child on earth. Surely He had guided the steps of the white kitten for the sake of the baby born in Bethlehem. Dani's father paused for a moment in his milking and thanked God on behalf of his little son.

Annette appeared in the kitchen shortly afterward to get breakfast and stood still in amazement at the sight of Dani in his nightshirt and overcoat watching over a white kitten. She was about to ask questions when Dani put his finger on his lips to ask her to be quiet, for he was very much afraid of waking the kitten. Then he tiptoed over to her, pulled her down on a chair, climbed onto her knee, and whispered the whole strange story into her ear.

Annette had no difficulty explaining it to herself. She believed that such a pure white kitten must surely have dropped straight from heaven. She sat down on the floor and gathered Dani and the kitten onto her lap, and here Grandmother found them half an hour later when she came in expecting to find her Christmas coffee steaming on the table.

4

The Quarrel Begins

Lucien lay under his large feather duvet and wished it was not time to get up. His bed was so warm and the air outside so cold. He sighed and cuddled down again under the bedclothes.

"Lucien!" His mother's voice sounded really angry, and Lucien jumped up in a hurry. This was the third time she had called him and he had pretended not to hear. He could still get up and be in time for school, although he would not have time to do the milking. But, after all, if he didn't do the milking, his mother would have to, and these days she did it more often than not.

"Other boys don't have to milk before they go to school," muttered Lucien as he buttoned his jacket, "and I don't see why I should always have to work harder than everyone else just because I don't happen to have a father."

He went downstairs looking sulky and defiant and sat down to gobble up his bread and coffee. His mother came in from the stable when he was halfway through.

"Lucien," she said sharply, "why don't you get up when I call you? It happens day after day! You're no help to me in the mornings at all. Your sister gets up early enough and goes off to work without any fuss. I know other boys have fathers, but we only have three cows and we can't live without them. You're a big, strong boy now and it's shameful that you should leave all the early work to me like this."

Lucien scowled. "I work at night," he whined. "I never get any play. I have to fetch in the wood, and I have farther up the hill to come than any of the others, and I fetch down the fodder for you and clean the shed on Saturdays."

His mother sniffed. "I've usually done most of it by the time you get home from school," she replied. "I know you don't get as much time in winter as other children, but I do all I can, and this early-morning milking is wearing me out. You're quite old enough to do it now, and in future you're to get up properly. Now hurry off or you'll be late for school."

Lucien struggled into his coat and turned away with a sulky good-bye. He unhitched the sled and went whizzing away into the frosty dark. Except for the smooth sound of the sled runners, the world was quite silent, as if it was holding its breath before the coming of dawn. Usually Lucien felt in awe of the greatness of it, but today he was too cross to think about it.

"It's so unfair," he muttered. "Everyone's against me. It's not my fault I don't get my lessons done properly. I'm always having to work at home. It's reading today, and I suppose I shall be bottom again, and that show-off Annette Burnier will be top. I bet she doesn't have to milk cows before school. Oh!"

He tried to stop, but it was too late; he had reached the fork in the path, and he had been so busy feeling cross that he had not looked where he was going. He had bumped straight into Annette's sled sideways on and sent her right into the ditch.

It was careless sledding, and Lucien, crimson in the face and truly upset, jumped off his sled to help, but Annette was before him. She had never liked Lucien much, and she was badly shaken. She turned on him, waist deep in snow, her eyes blazing.

"You great clumsy donkey," she shouted, half crying. "Can't you look where you are going? Look at my book—all my work is smudged and torn! I shall tell the master it's all your fault."

Lucien, who was never good at keeping his temper, lost it at once.

"All right," he shouted back. "There's no need to make such a fuss. I didn't do it on purpose. Anyone would think I'd killed you instead of tearing your old exercise book. It won't hurt you to lose your marks. I'm going on."

He jumped onto his sled and whizzed away, arriving just in time for school. Inside he felt really bad about it, but his manners were never very good at the best of times, and he tried not to think of what he had done.

"She's only got to get out," he muttered, "and I don't suppose she would have let me help her in any case. Thank goodness I'm in time for school. I've been late twice this week already."

But getting out of that snowdrift was a very different matter from getting in, and poor Annette had quite a struggle. By the time she had managed to get herself out and collect her books, she was really crying—crying with cold and shock and sore knees and, most of all, crying with rage. When she crept into school a quarter of an hour later, her eyes were red and her nose was blue and her poor raw hands and knees were grazed and bleeding. With her torn, wet books, she looked a sorry sight.

"Annette," said the master, quite concerned, "what has happened to you, my child?"

For a few seconds Annette fought hard with the temptation to tell tales, but the sight of Lucien sitting so smug and safe in his desk was too much for her.

"It was Lucien," she burst out angrily. "He knocked me into a ditch, and went off and left me. I couldn't get out." She stuffed her knuckles into her eyes and began crying again. She was really very badly shaken, and oh, so angry!

The class all felt sorry for her and angry with Lucien, who hung his head and looked very sullen indeed.

The master caned Lucien for behaving in such an unkind way, which cheered Annette up and made her feel much better. Later, when the marks were read out, Annette came out top and felt better still.

Lucien came out bottom and was told to stay in and do extra work after school. So he sat through morning school and lunchtime with the others, and came back to afternoon school and sat on alone when the others had gone. All the time the rage and hatred and bad temper in his heart were getting bigger and bigger till he felt as if he was going to burst.

At last he was let out from school and wandered up the hill dragging his sled behind him. What a terrible day it had been! His mother had been cross with him, Annette had told tales about him, the master had caned him, and he had come out bottom. Was ever a boy so badly treated?

The shadows on the fields were strangely blue that night. High up, the mountaintops were still sunlit, with ragged wisps of cloud trailing about them. The quietness of the mountains seemed to hold out its arms to Lucien. Children and Nature are very close together, and often Nature's silence can do more to heal angry, unhappy children than any human words can. So, as he trudged up the hill, Lucien's rage began to change to a sort of weary misery. Thinking he was alone, he stuffed his knuckles into his eyes and began to cry a little.

Then he suddenly discovered that he was not alone. He was again at the place where the path divided, and a little boy was standing in the snow looking up at him in great astonishment. A happy, rosy-cheeked, bright-eyed little boy, his fair hair stuck out like a thatch from under his woolly cap, his face glowing with good health and good humour.

It was Dani, making a snowman. He had just put on the head and was arranging the eyes. It was the best snowman Dani had ever made, and he was just about to fetch Annette to look at it.

"Why are you crying?" asked Dani.

"I'm not crying," retorted Lucien angrily.

"Ooh, you are," replied Dani, "and I know why. It's because the master caned you; Annette told us."

He did not mean to be cruel, for he was usually a kind little boy. But Lucien had been nasty to Annette, and that, to Dani, was quite unforgivable. Lucien's temper flared up instantly, and lifting his foot he kicked Dani's snowman into little bits. Dani lifted up his voice and gave a loud howl of alarm and disappointment.

Annette, crossing from the shed, saw what was happening in an instant. She flew down the path like a young tigress and slapped Lucien full in the face. Lucien lifted his hand to hit her back, but the sight of Monsieur Burnier coming out of the chalet with a bucket made him think better of it. Everything was clearly against him.

"Sneak! Telltale! Coward!" shouted Lucien. "Baby! Coming into school crying like that."

"Great, rough bully," shouted back Annette, "leaving me in the ditch like that, and then kicking poor Dani's snowman. He never did you any harm. Why can't you leave him alone? I'm jolly glad you were caned! Come on, Dani, come home."

She marched angrily off up the path, with Dani trotting behind her. At the door of the chalet she turned and noticed a patch of pink sky behind the far mountains. Once, Grandmother had taught her a text from the Bible, which said, "Do not let the sun go down while you are still angry."* She suddenly thought of it now. Well, there was still time — Lucien was still there. After all, it was nasty of her to have told tales. She hesitated.

But he'd been much worse than she had. It was up to him to say he was sorry. If she asked him to forgive her it would seem as if she was to blame, and of course she wasn't—oh, no, not in the least! She went in and slammed the door behind her.

Lucien went slowly home with his face stinging from that slap, more furious than he had been all day long. But, as he walked, he glanced up and noticed a wonderful thing. The clouds had come up in a purple bank, blotting out the mountain behind his home, but just in one spot they had broken, and in that gap Lucien could see the snowy crest, radiant with golden light.

He was used to winter sunsets, but the beauty of this one made Lucien catch his breath and look again. The pure, high radiance suddenly made his anger seem a poor, small thing, not worth hanging on to. How nice it would be to start again! There was still time to catch Annette if he ran.

But no! Annette was a show-off and would probably take no notice of him. And anyhow, why should he apologize to a girl?

So, because neither would be the first to forgive, the quarrel began—a quarrel that was to last for a

*Ephesians 4:26

very long time and was to bring with it a great deal of unhappiness for both of them.

As Lucien stood there thinking, a cloud blew across the gap, and the radiant mountaintop was hidden from view.

5

The Accident

Annette's birthday took place in March, and Dani made plans about it for weeks beforehand, for nothing pleased Dani so much as giving presents. Some people might have said his presents were not worth very much, but Dani thought they were beautiful. He kept them in a secret cupboard meant for storing wood. Annette knew that she must never go there, and pretended to think that it was full of wood chips for the stove.

Already the cupboard contained a family of fir cones, painted all different colors and arranged in a row. Father fir cone was red, Mother fir cone was green, and there were five little fir cones painted bright yellow. Then there was a beautiful picture Dani had drawn of Paquerette, the light brown cow, grazing in a field of enormous blue gentians nearly as big as herself. There was a pure white pebble and a little bracelet made from the plaited hairs of the bull's tail. And sometimes there was a chocolate stick, but it never stayed long because Dani loved chocolate sticks and usually ate them himself after a day or two.

But now the great day was nearly here, and tomorrow would be the real birthday. Dani's curly head was full of it, and as soon as Annette had gone to school, Dani explained his plan to Grandmother. She was sitting on the veranda in the spring sunshine, chopping dandelion leaves for that evening's soup, when her little grandson came up and rested his elbows on her knee.

"Grandmother," announced Dani, "I'm going up the mountain to where the snow has melted to pick soldanellas and crocuses for Annette's birthday. I will put them on the breakfast table with all my presents."

His grandmother, who hated him being out of her sight, looked doubtful.

"You are too little to go up the mountain alone," she replied. "The slopes are slippery and you will fall into the snowdrifts."

"Klaus will go with me," said Dani earnestly.

Grandmother chuckled. "A lot of good may she do you," she replied, and then gave a little shriek because Klaus, without the slightest warning, had leaped into Grandmother's lap and begun rubbing her white head against her, purring lovingly.

"Klaus knew we were talking about her," said

Dani. "She knows everything, and she is just telling you that she will look after me up the mountain."

He picked his kitten up around the middle, kissed Grandmother, and stomped off down the balcony steps, singing a happy little song. Crash went his hobnailed boots, and his voice rose loud and clear.

His grandmother strained her dim old eyes to watch him until he was out of sight, then she gave a little sigh and went on with her dandelions. He was growing so big and independent, and in a very short time he must start at the infant school. He was a baby no longer.

Dani trotted on up the slopes, and Klaus walked carefully behind him, for although she was a Christmas kitten she hated walking in the snow. It was a beautiful spring day and the snowdrifts on the mountains were beginning to melt. Already the fields were green beside the river in the valley, and the cows were grazing out of doors.

Klaus continued to pick her way until she reached the low stone wall at the edge of the field. On the other side of this wall was a rocky ravine with a rushing river at the bottom. In summer the rocks were like fairy gardens, with wild flowers growing all over them, but now they were bare and brown. Klaus sat on the wall and fluffed out her fur in the sunshine. Then she started to wash herself all over, which was unnecessary because she was already almost as white as the snow.

Dani wandered from yellow patch to yellow patch gathering flowers. The field was bright with pale mauve crocuses and bright primulas that followed the windings of the streams in the grass like little pink paths. Dani loved them, but what he loved best of all were the soldanellas. They could not even wait for the snow to melt, but pushed right up through the frozen edges of the drifts, their frail stems covered in ice. Their flowers, like fringed mauve bells, hung downward.

Dani loved all beautiful things, and in this field of flowers he was as happy as a child could be. The sun shone on him and the flowers smiled up at him, and Dani told himself stories about tiny goblins who lived in caves under the snow. Their beards were white and their caps were red and they were full of mischief. Sometimes if there was no one looking they came out and swung on the soldanella bells— Annette had said so.

For this reason he approached each fresh soldanella clump on tiptoe and kept his eyes fixed on their bowed heads. That was why he never heard footsteps approaching until they were quite close, and then he looked up suddenly with a little start.

Lucien stood close behind him, with a rather unpleasant look on his face and a strange gleam of triumph in his eyes.

Lucien had not forgotten the slap that Annette had given him when Dani had screamed for help. Ever since that day he had planned some revenge, and when he had seen Dani's little figure standing alone in the high pasture he had hurried to the spot. Of course he would not hurt such a tiny child, but it would be fun to tease and annoy him, and pay him back for telling tales. At least he could take his flowers from him.

"Who are you picking those for?" demanded Lucien.

"For Annette," replied Dani firmly. He had a feeling that Lucien would not like this answer, but Annette had told him that he must always speak the truth, even when he was frightened.

Lucien gave a horrid laugh.

"I hate Annette," he announced. "She is a proud, stuck-up show-off. But at school she is hopeless. The little ones in the infant school are better at sums than she is. She knows no more than her own cows. Give those flowers to me; she shall not have them!"

Dani was so shocked at this speech that he went bright pink and put his flowers behind his back. How could anyone hate Annette? Annette, who was so beautiful and so good and so clever and so wise. Dani, who had never heard of jealousy, could not understand it.

"You can't have them," said Dani, holding the bunch tightly in his small hands. "They are mine."

"I shall take them," replied Lucien. "You are only a baby and you can't fight against me. I shall do as I please to you. You are a little telltale and I shall pay you back."

He snatched the bunch roughly from Dani's grasp and flung them on the ground and trampled on them. Dani stared for a moment at the crushed soldanellas and bruised crocuses, and then burst into a loud howl. He had spent the whole happy afternoon gathering those flowers, and now they were all wasted. Then he flung himself on Lucien and began beating him with his small fists.

"I shall tell my daddy," he shouted. "I shall go straight home and tell him this very minute and he will come to your house and he will beat you. You are a cruel, wicked boy."

Now this was exactly what Lucien did not wish to happen, for, like most bullies, he was cowardly and was afraid of Dani's father. Dani's father was as tall and strong as a giant, and any ill treatment of his son would certainly make him furious. Lucien held Dani firmly by the wrists to stop him punching and looked around the field, wondering what he could do to stop the little boy from telling his father.

He suddenly spotted Klaus sunning herself on the wall, and he had an idea. He pushed Dani away and walked quickly towards the ravine.

Dani, who thought his tormentor had left him, wiped away the tears with the back of his hand and began picking fresh flowers as fast as he could. Lucien or no Lucien, Annette's birthday table must be bright and beautiful.

Suddenly Lucien's voice came ringing across the field. Dani looked up quickly, and what he saw made him feel quite sick for a moment. Lucien was standing by the wall, holding Klaus out at arm's length by the scruff of her neck—holding her right over the dark ravine with the rushing torrent of melted ice down below.

"Unless you come here at once and promise not to tell tales to your father," called Lucien, "I shall drop your kitten into the ravine."

Dani began to run, stumbling blindly over the

snowdrifts, but his legs were trembling and he could not run fast. The thought of Klaus being carried away helpless in that swirling brown water filled him with such horror that his mouth went dry and he could not cry out. He only knew that he must get there and snatch his kitten out of the grasp of that wicked boy and never, never let it go again.

Now let it be said here, right at the beginning of this story, that Lucien never for one moment meant to drop Klaus. He was unkind, and a bully, but he was not a murderer. But Klaus was not used to being held by the scruff of the neck, and after a moment or two she began to struggle. Finding that Lucien did not let her go, she struggled more violently, and then finally, getting frantic, she did what she had never done before. She put up her front paw and gave Lucien a sharp scratch.

Lucien, who was watching Dani's stumbling progress, was taken by surprise and let go. Klaus dropped like a stone into the ravine, just as Dani, white and tearful, reached the wall.

Dani did not hesitate a single moment. He gave a shriek like some small, terrified animal caught in a trap and hurled himself over the low wall. Lucien, quite paralyzed for a few seconds by what he had done, had time to grab hold of him and pull him back.

After that, everything happened in a few seconds. Klaus had not fallen into the water. She had stuck fast on a ledge of overhanging rock and clung there, mewing pitifully. An older child might have reached her safely and scrambled back, but Dani was only five. The surface of the rock was wet and Dani's feet slipped just as he reached his kitten. He gave another scream—a scream that haunted Lucien for years to come—and disappeared over the edge.

If Lucien had not been half stupid with panic, he would have scrambled down after him and peered over into the ravine. But he believed Dani must be dead, and to see the body of the child carried away by the water, down toward the waterfall, was more than he could bear. He sank down on the grass in a limp little heap and covered his face with his arm. Had Annette seen him at that moment, even she might have realized that Lucien had certainly been punished.

"Dani is drowned," he moaned over and over again. "I have killed him. What shall I do? Oh, what shall I do?"

Gradually a cowardly idea came into his mind, and he sprang up and looked around wildly. Time was getting on. People would soon come and look for Dani, and then they would find him and everyone would know that he was a murderer. No one so far knew that he had had anything to do with the accident, and if he hurried home and behaved as if nothing had happened, no one would ever know. He must escape.

He ran like a hunted rabbit into the shelter of the pinewood with his heart beating furiously and his head throbbing. He dared not go home just yet, but he made his way around by lonely paths, so that if anyone should see him coming it would look as though he had come in another direction. Every few minutes he thought he heard footsteps following and leaped around to look. But there was no one there.

At last he reached his own back door, and here he stopped. No, he could not go in. He could not face his mother, who believed in him, with that dreadful secret in his heart. Surely she would see it in his face. He could not look the same as before. He was a murderer.

Perhaps later he would summon up the courage to face her, but not yet, for his teeth were chattering, and she would ask what was the matter. In the meantime he must hide. He looked around wildly for some place and saw the ladder leaning against the barn where the straw was stored in the attic above the cowshed. Up the ladder went Lucien, and flinging himself face downward on the straw he sobbed as though his heart would break.

6

The Rescue

Grandmother finished shredding the dandelions and then, leaning heavily on her stick, went back to the house and sat down in her chair. She was very, very tired, and soon her head nodded onto her chest and she fell asleep.

Grandmother was more lame than ever by now, and nearly blind, and she was usually very tired, but she loved her two grandchildren greatly and was going to work for them as long as she possibly could. So she continued to cook with crippled hands and to mend with strained, aching eyes. Annette never realized, for she was only twelve and Grandmother never complained. If we work because we love someone, it doesn't seem too difficult.

Grandmother slept much longer than usual.

Annette had gone down to the village shop, and Papa was up in the forest cutting and stacking logs. She had meant to mend Dani's white woollen socks and put patches on the elbows of his blue jacket, but she was much too tired. She just folded her twisted old hands on her lap and went on sleeping—even the cuckoo jumped out of the clock and struck three without waking her.

It was nearly four when Grandmother woke and looked at the clock, and then she gave a little cry of alarm and surprise. Dani had gone out at half past two and had not yet returned. Where could he be?

"Dani," she called out sharply, for he might be hiding. Perhaps in a moment he would tumble out of the cupboard, as cheeky and mischievous as usual.

But there was no answer. Grandmother hobbled onto the veranda and shaded her dim eyes. Perhaps she would catch sight of him stomping home, and how she would scold him for being so late!

A figure appeared around the cowshed, but it was not Dani. It was Annette with her basket on her back and a long, golden loaf sticking out of the top of it. She had a half holiday from school and had been shopping. She waved to Grandmother and came running up the steps.

"Annette," said Grandmother, "take your basket off and go and search for your little brother. He went out to pick flowers nearly an hour and a half ago and he hasn't come back."

Annette let down her basket with a thump. She thought that her grandmother was rather fussy about Dani. What harm could come to him, wandering about in the fields where anyone he might meet knew and loved him?

"He will be up in the woods with Papa," Annette replied. "I'll go up and see in a few minutes. Let me have a piece of bread and jam first, Grandma. I'm hungry."

She broke off a thick hunk from the loaf and spread it with butter and jam while her grandmother went back to the balcony and peered up the path again. While she was eating, firm footsteps were heard down the hillside and Papa came into sight.

"Where is Dani?" cried Grandmother. "Hasn't he been with you, Pierre? Didn't you meet him up the mountain?"

"Dani?" repeated Papa in astonishment. "He hasn't been near me. When did he leave you, Mother?"

Grandmother stopped trying to hide her worry. "He left me over an hour and a half ago," she cried. "He and the kitten. They went out to pick crocuses in the field nearby. Something must have happened to him!"

Annette and her father looked at each other. Both were worried now, for the path from the forest led through the crocus fields, and Papa had seen no sign of Dani when he was on his way home. Annette slipped her hand into her father's.

"Perhaps he has wandered into the forest to look for you," she said comfortingly. "Let's go and look for him. Klaus will probably be about somewhere to show us which direction he's gone. Klaus hates long walks."

Together they set out up the hill toward the forest,

but they went in silence, for Papa was afraid to say what he was thinking. Spring brings certain dangers to mountains in Switzerland—swollen torrents and sudden falls of melting snow called avalanches—and Dani was such a tiny boy.

Grandmother, left alone, went indoors and prayed. As she prayed she saw a picture, for the less Grandmother saw with her real eyes, the more she saw with her mind. This time there seemed to rise before her the picture of a dark forest, with deep rushing streams, its paths rough with boulders and blocked with avalanches. Dani was running along this path with his hands full of crocuses, and beside him walked an angel with white wings, and in the shadow of those wings there was shelter and warmth and safety.

The words "the angels of little ones are always in the presence of the Father in heaven" came into her mind, and she got up from her knees feeling quite peaceful and began to get the evening meal ready.

There was still no sign of Dani or Klaus in the fields, nor at the edge of the pinewoods. Up and down Annette and her father searched, calling his name, but nothing answered except the echoes and the rushing of the torrent. Slowly the sun sank toward the mountain peaks and the shadows grew longer on the fields.

"Papa," said Annette suddenly, "I wonder if he has gone down to Lucien's house. I have seen Lucien talking to him once or twice. I will run down to their chalet and ask."

Over the snow drifts and grass she bounded, and

she reached Madame Morel's chalet in less than five minutes. The back door stood open, and Annette put her head around.

"Madame," she called, "Lucien! Are you there? Have you seen Dani?"

The house was silent and deserted, yet they could not have gone far, for they had left the door wide open. Annette was about to run across to the barns when she caught sight of Madame Morel's stout figure toiling up the track that led to their own chalet. Annette ran to meet her.

"Madame," she cried eagerly, catching hold of her hand, "have you seen our little Dani? He has run away, and we have not seen him for two hours. Do you think he might be with Lucien, and if so, where is Lucien?"

"He may well be," answered Madame Morel rather grimly. "I have just been down to your chalet to ask if you could give me any news of Lucien. The lazy boy should have been home long ago, and the cow is crying out to be milked. I shall have to do her myself, unless he has arrived while I was away. If so, he will have gone straight to the shed. Let's go across and see."

They went together over to the barn and opened the heavy wooden door. The red cow was stamping and twitching her tail, but there was no Lucien to be seen. Madame Morel turned away angrily and was just about to close the door when Annette seized hold of her sleeve and held up her finger.

"Listen," she whispered. "What is that noise up in the loft?"

They both stood listening hard for a moment. From the straw dump above them came the sound of a child crying.

Annette was up the ladder in an instant like a little wild cat, and Madame Morel lumbered up behind her. Both of them knew that something was desperately wrong, but Annette thought only of Dani and Madame thought only of Lucien.

"Lucien," cried Madame Morel. "My poor child, what is the matter? Are you hurt?"

"Dani," hissed Annette, seizing him by the arm and shaking him. "Where is he? What have you done with him? Give him back!"

Lucien cowered lower in the straw and shook his head violently. He was quite hysterical by now.

"I don't know where he is," he screamed. "It wasn't my fault."

"*What* wasn't your fault?" Annette screamed back, shaking him worse than ever. "Where is he? You do know. You're telling lies! Madame, make him speak the truth!"

Madame dragged Annette out of the way and knelt down by Lucien. Her face was very white, for by now she had guessed that some harm had come to Dani and Lucien knew of it. She pulled his face up from the straw and turned it toward her.

"Lucien," she commanded, trying to talk quietly, "speak at once. Where is Dani?"

Lucien stared at her wildly and saw that all escape was impossible.

"He's dead," he said with a hiccup, then began to cry again with his head buried in the straw.

Annette had heard but she did not move. For just a few moments she felt frozen all over. Her face was so white in the dim light that Madame thought she was going to faint. She tried to put her arm around her, but Annette sprang away. Then she spoke in a hoarse voice that did not sound like her own any longer.

"He must come and show us where," she said at last. "At least my father can carry him home. And later," she added, "I will kill Lucien."

Madame took no notice of the last part of this speech, but the first suggestion sounded sensible. She took her boy by the arm, dragged him to his feet, and almost carried him down the ladder.

"Come, Lucien," she urged at the bottom, "you must show us where Dani is, quickly. Otherwise, Monsieur Burnier will be here with the police to make you go."

This threat frightened a little bit of sense and reason into Lucien, and he set off up the hill as fast as he could go, sobbing all the time and protesting that it was not his fault. Madame Morel and Annette followed. Madame was sobbing as well, but Annette could not shed one tear, for she felt as if all her tears were frozen up by rage and misery.

They reached the wall very quickly and Lucien pointed into the darkening ravine. "He's over there, drowned in the torrent," he whispered, then flung himself down and buried his face in the grass. At this moment Monsieur Burnier appeared at the edge of the wood and hurried toward the little group.

He took no notice of Lucien but took one look at

his daughter and one look at the rocks. In that quick glance he saw something that none of the others had noticed—a shivering white kitten crouching on a ledge, right on the crest of the overhanging boulder. Once he had seen this, no more words were needed for the moment. He simply said, "I must fetch a rope," and ran down the mountain like a man being chased by wild beasts.

Grandmother was at the door of the chalet, and she too saw by the look on his face all that she needed to know at that moment. Without a word, she watched him pull down the climbing rope that hung on the wall and run away into the shadows.

"In the ravine," he suddenly called back, then he disappeared.

Grandmother, left alone, put on a kettle, fetched out old sheets, and filled a large stone hot water bottle, so as to be ready for anything. Then she sat down and shut her eyes and folded her hands. Once again she saw a picture of Dani, caught by the dark waters of the ravine, but the white wings of the angel stopped the current and Dani was caught up safely in his arms.

"God will put his angels in charge of you to protect you," whispered Grandmother, and she climbed the stairs to turn down his little bed and warm the blankets.

Dani's father was back with the rope in an amazingly short time, but to the watchers by the wall it seemed like hours. Nobody spoke as he secured it around a tree trunk and flung it over the boulder. Then, gripping it with his hands and knees, he backed himself down the slippery rocks and disappeared into the ravine. There, hanging in space, he dared to look down toward the rushing waters that must surely have carried away his child. What he saw sent a great rush of hope into his heart and a cry to his lips.

Grandmother had been right. The angels had taken care of Dani as he fell, and he had never reached the water at all. He had fallen onto a jutting-out boulder just below, and there he lay, flat on his back, with his leg doubled under him, waiting for someone to come and rescue him, and crying because he could not move.

The time had been long and Dani supposed he had been asleep, for he could never remember much about those two hours afterward. He really remembered only the moment when his father hovered over him like some great big bird, and then stopped by him and knelt on the rock at his side.

"Papa," whispered Dani, a little faintly, "where is Klaus?"

"Just above you," replied his father, checking everything in the little white face. "We will pick her up on the way back."

"Papa," went on Dani, "my leg hurts and I can't move. Will you carry me home?"

"Of course," replied his father. "That is what I came for. I'll carry you home at once." And he took his little son in his arms.

"But Papa," went on Dani's weak, worried voice, "can you carry us both, Klaus and me together? You won't leave Klaus, will you? It's time she had her milk and she will be very thirsty."

"Klaus shall go in my pocket," promised his father as he lifted the child very, very gently. Dani moaned, for his leg hurt when he moved. But he kept his eyes on his father's face and was really as brave as it is possible to be at five years old.

It was a long, slow journey back. Dani's father could not climb the rope with Dani in his arms. He had to scramble down to the edge of the torrent and pick his way along the side of it until they came to a part where the bank was less steep and he was able to make his way up. Dani fell into a sort of deep sleep and seemed to know nothing until his father laid him down on the grass beside Annette.

"Have you got Klaus in your pocket?" asked Dani, opening his eyes suddenly.

"I'm fetching her now," replied his father. Holding the rope, he slid to the edge of the precipice again and picked up the white kitten. Dani held out his arms and Klaus nestled down against his heart, purring like a little steam engine. Annette, for the first time in all that nightmare evening, burst into tears.

They laid Dani on a coat, and Madame Morel and Monsieur Burnier carried him slowly home down the mountain, while Annette came behind carrying Klaus. A sad little procession, and yet their hearts were full of grateful joy because Dani was alive and had spoken. That was enough for the moment.

No one, not even his mother, gave one thought to Lucien, who still lay under the wall, huddled down in the grass. When he lifted his head and found that he had been left alone with the night, he felt as though the whole world had turned its back on him and forgotten him. He got up, slunk home through the shadows, and crept, shivering, to bed, feeling the most lonely and miserable little boy in the whole world.

7

Annette Plans Revenge

Dani lay in his little bed between warm blankets, knowing very well that he was a tremendously important person and that anything he wanted would be fetched immediately. As this had never happened before, Dani was making the most of it.

Papa stood at the end of the bed watching him and telling him all the funny stories he liked best. Annette sat on one side of him with a chocolate stick in her hand. Klaus was curled up on his chest purring. Grandmother sat on the other side of his bed with a bowl of cherry jam, and every time he asked for it she gave him a spoonful! If his leg had not been aching so much Dani would have thought he was in heaven. Even so, the cherry jam didn't make the ache seem that bad.

"Papa," said Dani, for about the tenth time, "are you really sure Klaus isn't hurt?"

"Quite certain," answered his father. "She drank a whole dish of milk and ran upstairs with her tail up. Only healthy kittens would behave like that."

"Papa," went on Dani, opening his mouth like a baby bird for another spoonful of cherry jam, "it was Lucien who threw Klaus over the wall. It was very cruel of Lucien, wasn't it?"

"Very," replied his father, "and he shall certainly be punished." But Monsieur Burnier was too happy to have his son alive to think very much about Lucien. It was Annette, sitting quietly by with a chocolate stick in her hand, who thought most about Lucien.

I shall not be in a hurry, thought Annette to herself, *but I shall never, never forgive him as long as I live. One day I shall do something terrible to him. I shall never forgive him. Never.*

"'Nette," said Dani, "I want my chocolate stick, and then I want to go to sleep. And you must stay with me, 'Nette, because my leg hurts."

"Yes, Dani," answered Annette, handing him the chocolate stick. "I'll stay with you till you go to sleep."

Papa and Grandmother kissed him and left. Annette pulled his head down against her shoulder.

"Sing to me," commanded Dani. "Sing my favorite song."

It was about asking Father God to forgive sins and protect little children, and Annette didn't want to sing it with her heart so full of hatred and revenge.

But Dani insisted, so in the end she gave in and sang it rather sadly. By the time she finished, Dani was fast asleep, dribbling his chocolate stick onto the pillow. She lay down beside him, and once again she wept, for she was very tired and the relief had been great. But they were not only tears of joy, for we cannot be truly happy if we hate someone.

She got up with a sigh and went downstairs. Her father was out with the cows, which had never been milked so late in their lives and were mooing and stamping with impatience. Grandmother was preparing something to eat, for neither she nor Papa had had a bite since lunchtime. No one had had time to think of anything but Dani.

"He is asleep," said Annette, and she sat down and stared wearily at the stove.

"The doctor should be here soon," said Grandmother, "and then we shall have to wake him, poor little chap. Never mind, let him sleep while he can."

"Grandma," said Annette, looking up suddenly after a little silence, "Lucien must be punished. What is to be done to him? I can't think of anything bad enough that would pay him back for what he did to Dani."

Grandmother did not answer for a time. Then she replied, "Have you ever thought, Annette, that when we do wrong it often brings its own punishment without anyone else interfering?"

No, Annette had never thought about it at all.

"Think of Lucien's fright when he saw Dani fall," went on Grandmother. "Think how miserable and terrible he will be feeling tonight, and think of his shame and fear of others finding out what he did. And then think whether perhaps he has not been punished enough already, and whether we should forgive him and help him to start again."

Annette did not take much notice of Grandmother's words, except for one sentence. "Think of his fear of others finding out what he did." That was a splendid idea. She would make sure people *did* find out. Wherever she went she would tell everyone. She would tell it in the village and tell it at school until everyone would hate him for his wickedness.

Her thoughts were interrupted by a hurried knock at the door, and Lucien's big sister burst into the room. She had arrived home from the town across the mountain, where she worked, just in time to meet the slow little procession coming down from the fields. She had raced down to the village post office to phone the doctor, who lived five miles up the valley.

"Dr. Pilliard can't come," she panted. "He has gone to another village to a sick woman and he won't be home till midnight and the last train's gone. They say you must take Dani in the cart to the hospital tomorrow morning and he will see him there."

"Thank you, Marie," said Grandmother. "It was good of you to go for us." She turned back to the kitchen. But Marie stayed. She wanted to know what had actually happened.

"Tell me, Annette," Marie said, lowering her voice, "how did the accident happen? Why is my mother so silent and troubled?"

"It happened up the mountain," replied Annette shortly. "Lucien threw Dani's kitten over the ravine and Dani tried to rescue it. Lucien did not try to stop Dani at all. I shouldn't be surprised if he pushed him. I think Dani has broken his leg. He lay on the rocks for hours and Lucien never told anybody. He could have died."

Marie went quite pale with horror, for she had never been very fond of her younger brother. If she had been, perhaps Lucien might have turned out a better, kinder boy. Children who are not loved themselves often find it difficult to love others.

"He shall be severely punished," she said angrily. "I will see to it myself." Then she flounced out of the house.

Annette smiled. To turn his own family against Lucien was just what she wanted. She felt her revenge had begun.

There was nothing more to wait for now, so after a rather silent meal Annette dragged her way up to bed, tired and heavy-hearted. She lit a candle and stood looking at Dani through eyes that were misty with tears. He lay with his damp hair pushed back from his forehead and his arms flung out, and his usual peaceful look had gone. He was frowning even in his sleep, and now and then he moved his head restlessly and muttered troubled words.

Annette got into her bed by the window, but tired as she was, she could not sleep. She felt strangely alone. Then, to her joy, she heard slow, painful steps climbing the stairs and Grandmother came into her room. Grandmother hardly ever came upstairs

64

because it hurt her rheumatic legs so badly.

"Grandma," cried Annette, holding out her arms.

Grandmother said nothing for a time. She sat down on the bed and stroked Annette's head until the child stopped crying.

"Listen, my child," said Grandmother at last, "when Dani was a baby we took him to the church, and by faith we asked Jesus to look after him. Every day in prayer we have asked God to hold him safe in His arms, and even when Dani fell, God did not let go of him. His arms were underneath him all the time. Even if he had been killed he would have been carried straight home to heaven. So let us dry our tears and go on trusting God to hold onto Dani and do the very best for him."

"But why did God let Lucien hurt Dani so?" argued Annette. "Grandma, I hate Lucien so much I should like to kill him."

"Then you cannot pray for Dani," replied Grandma simply. "God is love, and when we pray we are drawing near to love, and all our hatred must melt away like the snow melts when the sun shines on it in spring. Leave Lucien to God, Annette. He rewards both good and evil, but remember, He loves Lucien just the same as He loves Dani."

Grandmother kissed her and went away, and Annette lay thinking over her words. The last remark she did not believe. It seemed impossible that even God should love cruel, ugly, stupid Lucien as much as good, sunny little Dani.

But the first part she knew to be true, and it troubled her. She could not really pray for Dani and go on planning how to hurt Lucien. The two just did not go together. She wanted to pray for Dani, but if she did, her hatred might disappear and she did not want that to happen at all—anyway, not before she had really had her revenge.

In the meantime she would let Grandmother do the praying and she would go on planning her revenge. Just as she decided this, Dani sat up in bed and started crying in a frightened, half asleep sort of way.

"Klaus," cried Dani. "Where is Klaus? She has fallen in the stream."

Annette ran over to him. "No, no," she murmured comfortingly, "she is here," She picked up the white purring ball of fur at the bottom of the bed and put it in Dani's arms. He fell back and went fast asleep again with his kitten sprawling across his chest.

Annette waited beside him for a few minutes until his breathing grew quiet and peaceful. Then she climbed into bed and fell asleep, too.

8

A Day of Escape

Lucien lay in bed in the dark with a hot, throbbing head and eyes that would not shut. Each time he closed them he saw Dani just disappearing over the cliff. And it wasn't an ordinary cliff. It was a dark, steep cliff that had no bottom. You just went on falling forever and ever.

Now and again he fell half asleep, but each time he awoke with a little cry of fear and his heart beating wildly, for his dreams were even worse than his thoughts. If only someone would come! It was so dreadful being alone. He wanted his mother, and he knew she had come in, for he could hear her moving about in the kitchen below. But he dared not call to her, for she must be so terribly angry with him that perhaps she was staying away on purpose. Besides, his sister might answer his call, and Lucien did not in the least want to see his sister. What she would say to him he dared not even imagine.

He began to think about tomorrow. He supposed he would have to go to school and Annette would have told everyone. Nobody liked him much in any case, because he was ugly, bad-tempered, and stupid, but now they would all hate him. No one would be friends with him, or want to sit next to him in class, or walk home from school with him.

He heard steps on the stair, and his mother came into the room. He sat up crying and held out his arms to her, but she did not come to him. Instead, she sat down on the bed and watched him with a worried look on her face.

In her heart she felt very sorry for him, and she longed to comfort him, but she was frightened. She was afraid of what the Burniers would do if Dani was badly injured—afraid of the law, afraid of the doctor's bills that she could not pay. She dared not seem too sympathetic in case it should be said that she had taken her son's side. Besides, she felt it was her duty to punish him somehow.

If she had been a more understanding woman she would have seen that no punishment from her was needed. She would have seen the long weeks of fear and misery, loneliness, and guilty shame that lay ahead of Lucien. She would have known that her part was to comfort him and help him through them as best as she could. But she was not an understanding woman.

"You are a naughty boy, Lucien," she said heavily,

"and I do not know what is going to happen. If that Burnier child is badly injured we shall be ruined. We shall have to pay all the bills, and we cannot possibly afford it. I expect we'll get the police after us. It's a terrible thing you've done, and I hope you are thoroughly ashamed of yourself."

Lucien was so very ashamed of himself that he didn't answer at all, which puzzled his mother very much for he was usually quick to answer back and to stick up for himself. A silent Lucien was indeed a new thing.

"Well," she said at last in a gentler voice, "we must hope for the best. Tomorrow you could go and tell the Burniers how sorry you are, and perhaps they will forgive you."

She waited for his reply, but none came, so she left the room feeling very troubled. She returned later with a bowl of hot soup. It might be wrong to comfort her son, but she could at least feed him.

Lucien took the bowl and tried to eat, but at the third mouthful he choked and handed it back to his mother. Then flinging himself down with his face buried in the pillows, he cried again as though his heart would break. His mother said nothing, for she did not know what to say, but she stroked the back of his head gently. As his sobs grew quieter she crept away and left him alone.

When he awoke next morning he could not remember what had happened, nor why his head ached and his eyes felt so hot and heavy. Then it all came rushing back, and he remembered something else, too. Today he had to go to school and face the other children.

Dani might have died in the night and they would all know it was his fault.

He decided he would not go. He would hide all day. It would not be too difficult. He would run up to the pinewoods and come back in the afternoon, and no one would ever know. His mother would think he had been at school and no one from school would ask questions. He lived too far up the valley, and anyway, who cared? Of course someone would find out in the end, but today was all that mattered at the moment. He might feel differently tomorrow, or Dani might be better. Anything might happen later on, but today he would run away and hide.

He got up and went downstairs. Marie was in the kitchen. She had already eaten her bread and drank her coffee and was getting ready to set out for the station. She tossed her head and turned away when Lucien came in, but Lucien did not look at her at all. He passed through the kitchen in silence and went across to the stable to help his mother with the early milking.

She looked at him anxiously when he came in, but he said nothing. Sitting on the stool by the stove eating his breakfast, he was still perfectly silent. At last he got up, put on his coat, kissed his mother goodbye without a word, and went off.

She stood watching him as far as the bend in the road and then waved to him. He waved back and waited around the corner until he was sure she had gone. Then, turning on his steps, he ran off up the hill as quickly as his legs could carry him.

He ran very fast and arrived breathless into the quiet coolness of the great pinewood that went around the mountain. Here he was safe, for it was still early in the morning, so he sat down and began to think.

It was a beautiful pinewood, and sap was bursting from the trees and streaming down their grey trunks. The scent of pine needles rose from the ground and the forest seemed full of peace and cool light. Lucien suddenly felt a tiny bit more cheerful.

He had no idea what he was going to do all day, and he had no food, as dinner was always provided for him at school. But this strange feeling of hope made him feel sleepy, and because he had not slept well the night before, he stretched himself on the ground and fell into a deep sleep. He slept on until the sun was high overhead and the children down in the school were coming out to their dinners. Then he woke up and wanted his dinner, too.

But there was none to be had here in the forest, so he got up and wandered on up the hill, wondering whether some kind farmer in one of the higher chalets might give him a drink of milk. As he wandered he stuck his hands in his pockets and found his knife. He took it out. He sat down on a log, picked up a piece of wood, and began whittling away at it with the knife. He had often whittled at bits of wood, though he had never made anything properly. But now, with nothing to do, he decided to try to carve out the shape of a chamois, one of the wild mountain goats that live on the high precipices. He started off idly, chipping away.

Very gradually it began to take shape under his fingers, and a strange excitement took hold of him. For the first time he forgot his misery and became absorbed in what he was doing. He could see the creature in his mind's eye, and as he thought about it, so he shaped it.

Lucien held it out at arm's length to inspect it. It was not perfect, though it was very definitely a chamois and he had no idea how good it was. But for the first time since the accident he felt almost happy. He had found something he could do. Though he was stupid, he could carve, and now he would not mind being alone again. When the other children didn't want him he would come out to a quiet corner of the woods and see beautiful things and carve them. While he carved he could forget, and that was what he wanted more than anything. Whatever happened, he could come away by himself and forget.

He climbed up the slope and looked down over the forest to the valley below. The sun was moving toward the western mountains, and far beneath he could see little dark specks running in all directions. The children were coming out of school. In another quarter of an hour or so it would be safe to go home.

He walked slowly back through the pinewood, for he must not get back too soon. The sun was shining on the other side of the valley now, and the pinewood was cool and dark. Lucien kept his hand in his pocket with his fingers closed tightly over the rounded body of his chamois. It was a satisfying feeling.

He wondered rather dully what he would hear

when he got home. Dani might have died, but Lucien pushed that thought away from him, for he dared not face it. He was probably just badly hurt, and into Lucien's mind there came a picture of Dani's white, scared little face looking up from the grass.

If only he could do something to make up for it, but he could think of nothing.

He walked into the chalet a little sheepishly, and his mother, at the sink, looked at him anxiously. She waited a little while for him to speak, but at last, unable to wait any longer, she began to question him.

"Well," she began, "how did you get on at school today?"

"All right, thank you," answered Lucien.

"I've been down to inquire at the Burniers'," went on his mother, "and Annette and Monsieur Burnier have taken Dani to the doctor in the cart. They will not be back till late. The grandmother spoke very kindly, Lucien. They are good people and I think they will forgive you and not make the trouble you deserve."

Lucien did not reply. The grandmother might forgive him, but he knew quite well that Annette never would.

"Did the schoolmaster know of what happened?" asked his mother after a pause.

"Yes," replied Lucien.

"Did he say anything about it?" went on Madame.

"No," answered Lucien.

His mother was puzzled. She had had a miserable day thinking of what sort of a time her son might be having at school, but nothing seemed to have happened. He even looked slightly more cheerful than he had in the morning.

"I'm going over to milk the cows, Mother," said Lucien, and he crossed to the stable with a sigh of relief. The stable was a refuge where he could get away from his mother's questions, and where the cows thought none the worse of him. He started quickly, and then, tilting the bucket, drank about a pint of the warm, frothing milk straight off and felt better. He had had nothing to eat or drink since breakfast.

Tonight he would save some of his supper, and tomorrow he would go back to the woods again and spend another quiet, hidden day. He would do it every day until he was found out . . . and that might not be for a long time.

He took as long as he could over the milking and then wandered back into the house carrying the buckets. He reached the door at the same time as his sister, who had hurried up the hill and was flushed and out of breath.

"You little coward, Lucien," she exclaimed as she saw him. "Fancy missing school like that! What has he been doing all day, Mother? You should have made him go!"

Her mother turned around indignantly. "What are you talking about, Marie?" she asked sharply. "Of course he's been to school. He's only just come in. Leave the poor child alone and get on with your work."

"Indeed," exclaimed Marie. "Well, if he's only just

come in, I should dearly like to know where he's come from. I happen to have met the schoolmaster on my way up from the station. He was weeding his vegetable patch. He looked over the fence and called out to me. 'Where's Lucien?' he asked, 'and why has he not come to school? Is he not well?' I answered, 'He's well enough, and he shall come tomorrow if I have to drag him!' So now you know, Lucien! Goodness knows where you've been today, but tomorrow I shall take you to school myself."

"Fancy you lying to me like that, Lucien," cried his mother angrily. "You *are* a wicked boy. I do not know what to do with you. The master must deal with you." Because she was so worried, and because her boy had deceived her, she threw her apron over her face and began to cry.

Lucien sat down by the stove in bitter, sullen silence. Everyone and everything seemed against him. His only hope of escape had been taken from him. Tomorrow he would have to go to school and Annette would be there. If he had gone today she would not have been there.

He picked up a large wood chip and began whittling away with his knife, and once more his fingers felt for the wooden chamois in his pocket.

9

A Visit to the Hospital

Dani lay in the cart on a sack stretched across a soft mattress of hay and gazed up at the blue sky, where tiny, white, woolly clouds floated by. He would have liked to look over the sides of the cart, but this was impossible, for he could not sit up. So he looked at the sky instead, and Annette described the scenery and what was happening as they went along. Dani's leg ached badly, which made him rather bad tempered. When the cart jolted he squealed, but Annette spoke to him soothingly to calm him down, and it was still nice to feel so important.

"We are at the top of the village now, Dani," said Annette, "just passing the church, and there is Emil the dustman's son driving the cows out of the churchyard. Some naughty person must have left the gate open."

"Are the cows trying to go into church?" enquired Dani with interest.

"No," replied Annette. "They were trying to jump over the wall, but it was too high. They were jumping over the gravestones instead. Here we are at the infant school, Dani, and there is the teacher scrubbing her steps. I suppose it is her cleaning day and she has given all the infants a holiday. I wish the schoolmaster had cleaning days. Oh! Here is the teacher coming toward the cart. She has seen us and I expect she wants to know how you are. And here come Madame Pilet and Madame Lenoir. They have seen us, too. They were washing their clothes in the fountain."

Annette was right. They certainly wanted to know how Dani was, for in a tiny village news travels fast and is much talked about and long remembered because there is so little of it. The postman's wife had heard some of the story from Lucien's sister when she phoned for the doctor, and the station master's wife had heard the rest from Marie while she waited for the early train, and by now everyone was talking about it and everyone wanted to find out more.

So Madame Pilet and Madame Lenoir left their husbands' shirts bubbling like white balloons in the fountain while Madame Durez, who kept the village shop, left her counter and came running out with two customers behind her. The teacher left her scrubbing bucket to get cold, and they all crowded around the cart and stood on tiptoe to stare at Dani, lying flat on his back on his hay mattress—a little paler than usual, but otherwise quite cheerful and pleased to see them.

"Ah, the little cabbage," cried the teacher, throwing up her hands. "You must tell us about it, Annette." Although they had all heard the story once and repeated it to somebody else, they were all ready to listen again. So Annette told them about it, and they shook their heads a great deal and clicked their tongues. They were all very angry with Lucien.

"He is a wicked boy," said the infant school teacher. "I shall warn the little children not to have anything to do with him!"

"And I shall not allow Pierre to play with him," said the postman's wife. "He has a cruel heart. You can see it in his face. I feel sorry for his mother, having a child like that." She thought proudly of her own cheery, freckle-faced son, who was one of the best-loved boys in the village.

Dani's father flicked his whip rather impatiently and called back that they must not keep the doctor waiting. The women stood back and the cart lumbered on slowly over the cobblestones. Then they all drew together again and started talking in the middle of the road with their heads very close together.

The cart jolted on and the sun rose higher. The horse did not mind in the least keeping the doctor waiting, and Annette had plenty of time to describe the scenery to Dani as they made their slow way to town.

"The river is almost in flood, Dani," remarked Annette. "It's because the fine weather has melted the snows so fast. The water is right over the pine-tree roots, and here a tree has fallen right across like a bridge. Oh, Dani! There is a little grey squirrel wondering whether to run along it or not."

"Where?" cried Dani, and he forgot and tried to sit up, but fell back with a squeal of pain.

"You can't see," Annette warned him. "Anyhow, the squirrel has run back into the wood. We are getting near the station now, Dani, and there are three cows on the platform waiting to be put on the train."

The journey passed pleasantly. At last houses began to appear, and Annette told Dani they were coming into the town.

"Tell me about the shops," exclaimed Dani eagerly.

He had been to the town only three times in his short life and thought it was the most wonderful place in the world.

It wasn't much of a town, really, for there was only one narrow street of shops—but they were very nice shops. There was the cake shop with its windows packed with flat fruit tarts and piles of gingerbread cut into every shape imaginable, and the clothes shop with a display of embroidered national costumes. Best of all was the wood-carver's shop with its rows of carved cuckoo clocks and the old men who opened their mouths wide and cracked nuts in their wooden teeth. At last Father drove up in front of the hospital.

It was only a little hospital, really, but to Annette and Dani it seemed enormous. The patients all lay out on sunny balconies, and the door was wide open. Papa jumped down from the driver's seat, tied the reins to the fence, and went in. A few minutes later he returned with two men and a stretcher.

Dani, on his stretcher, was laid on a wooden bench in the outpatients' hall, with Papa sitting at his head and Annette at his feet. The quiet strangeness of the place and the odd, clean smell made them all go very quiet, so Dani watched the nurses instead. They wore long, white aprons and lace caps. Dani thought they looked exactly like the angels in Grandmother's big picture Bible.

They waited for a very long time. Papa and Annette nodded and dozed. Dani flung his arms above his head and fell into a deep sleep.

He was woken by the doctor, who appeared very suddenly and seemed in a great hurry. He was an elderly man with a large, black beard and a gruff voice. Annette felt afraid of him.

Everything seemed to happen very quickly after that. Dani was hustled off on a trolley to have the bones in his leg photographed, which was interesting, and he wanted to know whether he would be allowed to keep the photograph to hang up in his house. Then he was trundled back, and the doctor pulled the bad leg until Dani screamed with pain. Then the photographs were brought along, not looking in the least like Dani's legs.

But the doctor seemed pleased with them. He studied them deeply and nodded his head wisely. Then he turned to Papa and remarked, "This child should stay in the hospital. He has broken his leg very badly."

But Papa refused completely. He was not going to leave his little son to this man with his black beard and rough hands.

"We will look after Dani at home," he said firmly. "Surely that is possible?"

The doctor shrugged his shoulders. "It is possible," he replied, "but I think he would be better here. I cannot come so far. You would have to keep bringing him in."

"I don't mind bringing him in," said Papa stubbornly, and Annette put her little hand into his big one and gave it a squeeze. She, too, wanted Dani at home.

The doctor shrugged his shoulders again and spread out his hands. Dani was once more trundled off by a nurse in a great hurry, and this time he did not come back for more than half an hour.

When at last he was returned to them, he looked sleepy and strange and could remember absolutely nothing but a funny smell. It was Annette who discovered that he had on a big white plaster from his waist downward. She pointed it out to Dani, who stared down at himself in astonishment.

"Why have I got to wear these hard white trousers?" he asked at last. Then, without waiting for a reply, he said that he did not like the doctor's big, black beard and he wanted to go home.

Annette did not like it either, and they all wanted to go home—Annette because she was hungry, Dani because he was tired, and Papa because he was thinking about his cows.

When the doctor came back with a second photograph, Dani and his family were nowhere to be seen. In the far distance a sprightly horse was making her way home as fast as possible, pulling a hay cart and three passengers behind her. They had completely forgotten to ask when they should bring Dani back again, or for how long he had to wear his plaster.

They reached home at five o'clock and Dani was put to bed on the sofa, so that he wouldn't feel lonely, and Annette slept on a mattress beside him in case he should wake in the night and want her. Here Dani stayed for weeks with his leg on a pillow, and everything was arranged around him.

Annette stopped going to school altogether for the time being, and almost became Dani's slave. She told him all her stories over and over again and played games with him all day long. Grandmother cooked wonderful little meals in the kitchen to tempt the appetite of the "poor little sick boy" whose appetite didn't need tempting at all, for he was almost as jolly and cheery and hungry on his couch as he was off it. When Annette was busy, he would lie flat on his back on the veranda bed and sing like a happy lark.

He certainly had everything to make him happy; the village saw to that. They had loved his pretty, delicate mother who had grown up amongst them, and when she died they were all prepared to love her children—especially Dani, who had eyes as blue as forget-me-nots and a voice like a bird and was altogether as adorable as a five-year-old can be.

Dani, who had always taken love for granted, was not spoiled by it. He was just pleased and excited, for with so many wonderful presents and visits, he hardly missed his freedom at first.

The village children wandered up the mountains in search of the first alpine flowers for him until the table by his bed looked like an alpine flower garden. Because Dani loved to see them, Grandmother cheerfully put up with the noise and the muddy boots until the veranda, out of school hours, became a sort of public playground where Dani was in charge.

Then there was the schoolmaster, who sent fascinating picture books, and the innkeeper who sent brown speckled eggs, and the baker who made golden doughboys with currant eyes and candied peel buttons. He used to slip them in Annette's bread basket with a wink, and that was why Dani always insisted on unpacking the shopping-basket himself. He never knew what he might find—and whatever it was, he was quite certain it was for him.

But the postman was best of all. The Burnier family hardly ever received a letter, so the postman himself decided to write Dani a picture postcard each week, and trudged up the hill to deliver it himself. He came a different day each week, so every morning Dani got excited in case he should come.

The postman was never in a hurry, and always saw to it that the postcard was at the very bottom of the sack. He enjoyed Dani's squeals of excitement as he burrowed among the letters and read the names on all the cards in search of his own. And if the post that day was a little marked and crumpled, no one minded or asked questions.

10

Lucien Makes a Friend

Just as the village supported Dani and did all they could to comfort him, they also shunned Lucien, and did all they could to show how much they despised him.

For a few days he was really tormented. The schoolmaster made a speech about him in school, showing everyone what a bully and coward he was. The children chased him out of the playground and threw mud at him. But they soon gave that up and simply settled down to ignore him. When teams were picked he was always left till last. There was one extra single desk in the classroom, which he had to sit in. Everyone else sat in pairs.

Even the tiny children got out of his way, for their mothers had warned them to have nothing to do with him. "He is a cruel bully and may harm you as he harmed little Dani Burnier," they said. The little ones looked on him as some kind of monster and ran away whenever he came near them.

Down at the village, the shopkeepers handed over the things he bought without speaking to him. The milkman never chatted with him, and the grocer's wife never slipped trimmings of gingerbread into his hand as she did for the other children. They never spoke unkindly to him; they just took no notice of him.

Lucien, who was too shy to try to do anything to make them like him, drifted into a lonely little world of his own. He walked to and from school alone, he shopped alone, and in the playground he usually played alone. It was not that the children would not have him, for children forgive and forget quickly. It was simply his shame that kept him from joining in. Always he saw their dislike of him in their faces and imagined they were thinking of Dani. Gradually he grew to be afraid of them, from the milkman right down to the youngest child in the school.

Lucien himself was always thinking of Dani. The thought haunted him, and he longed to ask Annette what the doctor had said. But Annette had neither looked at him nor spoken to him since the day of the accident, and he dared not speak to her.

At home his mother found him more silent but more hard-working, for he had suddenly discovered that only by hard work could he forget his loneliness. Instead of being lazy like he used to be, he started working very hard on the farm. His mother praised him loudly, and his sister became kinder, for she herself was a hard-working girl and Lucien's laziness had always annoyed her greatly.

There was one place, and one only, where Lucien was completely happy, and that was in the forest. Here the kindly trees shut him in, and the world that disliked him was shut out. Here Lucien fled whenever he had any spare time. Squatting against a tree trunk or boulder, he would carve away at his little figures and forget everything else in the joy of carving. Sitting beneath the pine trees, he would feel the sun on his hair and hands as he worked, and the peace and beauty of the forest in early summer soothed and comforted him.

High up on the borders of the forest there stood a small chalet where a very old man lived by himself. He had retired there long ago and lived alone with his goat, his hens and his cat. He was a strange old man and everyone in the village was afraid of him. He didn't come down to the village to shop very often, but when he did, the children ran away from him. They called him "the old man of the mountain." Some said he was a miser, some that he was hiding from the police, and others that he was crazy and bad. Whatever the real reason, no one had ever been inside his home, and no one ever passed that way after dark.

Lucien had wandered farther than usual up the mountain one half holiday from school, and sat as usual working hard on his carving. He was carving a squirrel holding a nut between its paws when he suddenly became aware of heavy breathing behind him.

He turned quickly to see the old man of the mountain looking over his shoulder.

He was certainly a terrifying sight. His huge, tangled, grey beard covered his chest, and his hooked brown nose made him look like some fierce bird of prey. But as Lucien gazed up, startled, into his eyes, he noticed that they were bright and kind and full of interest, and he decided not to run away after all. Besides, his great loneliness made him less afraid than he would have been otherwise. This old man might be odd, or even wicked, but at least he knew nothing about what Lucien had done.

So he said, "Bonjour, Monsieur," as boldly as he could and waited to see what would happen next.

The old man put out a hand like a brown claw and picked up the little carved squirrel. He examined it and turned it over several times, then he remarked, "You carve well for a child. Who is your teacher?"

"Monsieur, I have no teacher. I taught myself."

"Then you yourself are a good teacher, and you deserve proper tools. With a little training you might start to earn your living. This squirrel looks almost as if it is alive."

"Monsieur, I have no tools, and I don't have the money to buy them."

In reply the old man beckoned with his claw-like hand. Lucien, feeling like someone in a dream, got up and followed him through the dim wood. They climbed some way in silence until they came to the borders where the old man's tiny chalet stood.

There was no outhouse except for a wooden barn where the hens roosted, and the goat shared the kitchen with the old man. So did the ginger cat who sat washing himself in the sunshine. The bedroom was also the hayloft, and the old man slept on sacks laid across the goat's winter food supply of hay.

The kitchen and living room were poorly but strangely furnished. There was a stove, a milking bucket and stool, a table, one chair, and a cheese press. All around the walls, out of reach of the goat, were shelves covered with carved wooden figures— some beautiful, some ugly, but all the work of a real artist.

There were bears and cows and chamois and goats, St. Bernard dogs and squirrels. There were little men and women, gnomes and dwarfs, and dancing children. There were boxes with alpine flowers carved on their lids, and dishes with flowers carved around the rim. Best of all there was a Noah's ark with a stream of tiny animals marching in. Lucien could not take his eyes off it. He just stared and stared.

"It's just a hobby of mine," said the old man. "They keep me company on winter evenings. Now, boy, if you will come and visit me from time to time, I will teach you how to use the tools."

Lucien looked up eagerly. His whole face was alive, and he no longer looked ugly.

"Did you say, Monsieur," he asked hesitatingly, "that perhaps I might soon earn my living?"

"In time," said the old man, "yes. I have a friend who sells woodcraft at a good price. He sells many of my little figures, but some I get fond of and prefer to keep. In a short time he would start selling your best work for you. You will do much better with my tools than with your knife."

Still Lucien gazed up at him. His heart was singing with thankfulness because this old man seemed to care for him and wanted to take an interest in him. Here at last was somebody whom he needn't be afraid of, and who thought well of him. He grabbed hold of the old man's hand.

"Oh, thank you, Monsieur," he cried. "How very good you are to me!"

"Zut," said the old man. "I am lonely, and I have no friends. We can carve together."

"And I, too, am lonely and have no friends," replied Lucien simply.

As Lucien walked home through the forest, his brain was full of ideas, but there was one big idea more important than all the others. He would make a Noah's ark for Dani like the old man had done, with dozens of tiny figures—lions, elephants, rabbits, camels, and cows, and Mr. and Mrs. Noah. When it was quite perfect he would walk around to the Burniers' chalet and give it to Dani as a peace offering. Surely no one could give Dani a better present than that! And after that, perhaps they might even allow him to be just a tiny bit friendly with Dani again.

His heart beat fast at the very thought of it. For two whole hours he had been completely happy, and his happiness lasted all the way through the forest until the trees parted and he saw the village below him. Tomorrow he would have to go back to school. Tomorrow he would feel lonely and frightened again. But today he had found a friend.

Three times a week after school Lucien bounded through the quiet pine forest and sat on the step of the old man's chalet and worked on his Noah's ark. It was a wonderful thing to use tools with their sharp blades and easy curves—very different from his old penknife.

The old man marveled at the boy's skill. The Noah's ark family grew and grew. Every visit Lucien made, he thought of some new animal to carve, and the procession grew longer and longer.

There was another excitement for Lucien just about then. An inspector came to school and set up a handcraft competition for the children. The girls were to see who could enter the best piece of knitting, needlework, or lacemaking, and the boys the best piece of wood carving. Many of them whittled away at wood in their spare time, and some were becoming quite skilful.

"But no one is as skilful as me," whispered Lucien to himself as he plodded home alone. "I shall win the prize, and then they will know that I can do something well, even if I am stupid at lessons, and even if no one will play with me."

Lucien sang on his way home that day. He saw himself walking up for his prize in front of the amazed school. Perhaps they would like him better after that.

He would carve a horse with a flowing mane, in full gallop, with its tail outstretched and its nostrils dilated. Lucien loved horses. The old man had carved one like that and Lucien had admired it greatly. The Noah's ark would be finished very soon and then he could start on his little horse.

He ran straight up to the old man's house to share the news. The old man was pleased and as sure as Lucien was himself that he would win the competition.

"But why try a horse?" he asked. "You could enter your Noah's ark. It is very well done for a boy of your age."

Lucien shook his head. "That is a present," he said firmly.

"A present? Who for? Your little brother?"

"For a little boy who has hurt himself and cannot walk."

"Indeed? How did he do that?"

"He fell over the ravine."

"Poor little chap. How did that happen?"

Lucien did not answer for a moment, but the fact that this old man had become friends with him and been so nice to him made him want to speak the truth. He looked up at last and said, "It was my fault that he fell. I dropped his kitten over and he tried to get it."

He could have bitten his tongue out as soon as he said it, for he felt sure the old man would hate him now and drive him away like everybody else.

But he didn't. Instead, the old man said very gently, "So that is why you have no friends?"

"Yes."

"And are you hoping to make things right with this child by making this toy for him?"

"Yes."

"You are doing a good thing. It is hard work to

win back love. But don't give up. Those who perse-
vere find more happiness in earning love than they
do in gaining it."

"I don't quite understand you," said Lucien
thoughtfully.

"I mean that if you spend your time putting the
love of your heart into what you do for those who
are not your friends, you may often be disappointed
and discouraged. But if you keep on trying you will
find your happiness in loving, whether you are loved
back or not. You may think it strange that I who live
alone and love no one should say all this to you, but
I believe it all the same."

That evening the Noah's ark was finished. Lucien,
with a flushed face and a hammering heart, set off
for the Burniers' chalet to leave it on his way home.

When he came within sight of the chalet, he hid
behind a tree in panic. What would he say? How
would he break the silence? If he could see Dani
alone it would be easier, but Annette was always
with him out of school hours.

Surely they would forgive him when they saw the
Noah's ark! If only they would forgive him and give
him a chance, he would gladly spend the rest of his
life trying to make up for it. Struggling between hope
and fear, Lucien came out from behind his tree and
walked toward the chalet.

Annette was sitting alone outside.

Lucien swallowed hard, walked up to her, and held
out the Noah's ark.

"It's for Dani," he whispered, and the words
seemed to stick in his throat. Looking down at the

ground, he held up the box to Annette.

"How dare you come here!" she burst out. "How dare you offer presents to Dani! Go away. And don't you ever come here again!"

As she said it, she kicked the Noah's ark with all the strength of her young legs into the woodpile below her. All the little animals lay scattered on the logs.

Lucien stared at her for a moment, then he turned and ran as fast as he could. All his efforts had been for nothing. He would never be forgiven. It had all been one long waste of time.

Then the old man's words came into Lucien's mind like a tiny ray of light in his angry, bitter heart.

"Those who keep trying find more happiness in earning love than in gaining it."

Perhaps it was true. He had certainly not gained anything, but at least he had been happy making the Noah's ark and thinking of Dani's pleasure. Perhaps, if he persevered and went on putting his love into his work, someday someone would accept it and love him for it.

He did not know. But he decided not to give up just yet.

11

A Trip to the High Pastures

Dani's leg was very slow in healing. Many times the doctor climbed the mountainside to visit him, but he seemed worried and puzzled. The time came for Dani to go back to the hospital and have the plaster taken off. It was then that the doctor broke the news to Dani's father that, as he had feared all along, Dani would not ever be able to walk properly. His bad leg was much shorter than his good one.

Feeling very sad indeed, Monsieur Burnier went to the carpenter and asked him to make a tiny pair of crutches. Then he visited the cobbler with a pair of Dani's boots and asked him to make one sole an inch and a half thicker than the other one.

The carpenter and the shoemaker were very upset. The carpenter carved little bears' heads on the handles of the crutches to make Dani smile, and the cobbler returned the boots stuffed with chocolate sticks, and in both cases their efforts were a great success. Dani looked upon his crutches as a new toy and was really impatient to try them out.

For a day or two he hopped about like an excited grasshopper in front of the house Then he heard his father say that he was going to take his cows up the mountain to feed in the high pastures. Dani sat down and cried loudly, because he suddenly realized that, even with his nice bear crutches and his new boots, he could no longer follow the cows up the mountain.

Dani did not often bellow, but when he did, he really did! Annette, Monsieur Burnier, and Grandmother all rushed for the woodpile where Dani was crying, and they all started shaking him and kissing him at once. Klaus, who hated lots of noise, arched her back and hissed.

When at last they understood the reason for Dani's unhappiness, they all tried to make lots of comforting plans. In the end it was decided that Dani should go down to the marketplace in a little wooden cart to watch the cows gather together, and afterward he would drive up behind the herd in the horse cart, sleep the night in the hay, and come down next day. Annette would go with him, while Grandmother and Klaus stayed at home and kept house.

The great day dawned clear and blue, and Dani woke early with a feeling that something wonderful was going to happen. When he remembered what it was, he tried to yodel, which he couldn't do at all, and then dragged Klaus into bed with him and began to tell her all about it. But Klaus was not interested and struggled out again, and went with her tail in the air to catch mice on the woodpile.

An hour later Dani was curled up in the wood cart and Annette was taking him down to the village. Long before they reached the marketplace they heard the clanging of cowbells, the mooing of frightened cattle, the shouting of men, and the shrill screams of excited children. When they turned the corner by the fountain and bumped down the shallow steps, what a sight greeted them!

The market was a solid mass of cows and calves all pressed together. They all wore clanging bells and tossed their heads nervously. Here and there cows broke loose and jumped on each other, and over by the grocer's shop a crowd of young men was shouting at a young bullock who was trying to put his horns through the shop window. In and out among their legs swarmed the children, for this was a great holiday—school was closed.

In Switzerland, when the grass begins to grow long in the fields, the cows go up the mountains for the summer and feed in the high pastures while the hay ripens in the valleys. The farmers go up and live with them, while the women and children stay behind. On the day when they all set out, the cows are gathered together before starting on their different paths, and the children follow their own cows up to the high pastures and spend the day in the mountains, settling the cows into their new homes.

When Dani arrived in the marketplace people

gathered all around him. Except for his journey to hospital, this was his first public appearance in the village, and everyone wanted to look at him. All the children wanted to pull his cart, and all the women wanted to kiss him. What with the cows and the crowds and the cobbles, it was a wonder he wasn't tipped right out.

Time was getting on, and the procession had to start moving. The farmers were drawing their leaders out of the crowd, each group shoving its way out after them. The group leader wore a bigger bell than the rest, and was followed by all the others.

Monsieur Burnier was drawing out his leader by the collar, and his few cattle were making their way out from the crowd as best as they could. He walked up to Dani's cart with his hand on the cow's neck. "The mule cart is waiting around the back of the cobbler's shop," he said, "so put Dani into it, Annette, and we will make a start."

He went off, rounded up his cows, and set off up the steep steps behind the clock tower looking like a pied piper with a stream of children following him. All the children liked Monsieur Burnier.

Soon the mule cart caught them up, with Annette holding the reins and clicking her tongue. Dani lay in the back holding his crutches, which he had brought to show to the people in the village, and shouting at the top of his voice.

Dani never forgot that ride up the mountain. One of the bull calves, called Napoleon, grew tired and started dropping behind, so Dani leaned over and put his hand on his collar and pulled him alongside the cart.

His father looked back and smiled. "He's tired, poor young thing," he said. "You'd better take him in the cart with you, Dani."

Father lifted the wobbly-legged creature into the cart, and Dani flung his arms round his woolly neck and shrieked for joy. It was a beautiful calf with gentle eyes, silky ears, and pale, stubby curls on its forehead. They sat watching the forest together, sniffing the scent of the pine trees.

By the time they came out of the forest they had climbed so high that they could see right over the green mountains that surrounded the valley to the snow-capped ranges beyond, where the snows never melt. Dani lay back, counting the white peaks, and imagined himself in heaven. Then, to make his happiness complete, Annette suddenly produced a long twisty roll and a hunk of cheese and told him to sit up for his dinner. He sat nibbling one end of the hard golden crust while the calf put out its pale pink tongue and licked the other end.

Annette left the mule to make its own way while she wandered up and down the slopes picking the alpine flowers that grew in the high pastures as a present for Grandmother. It occurred to Dani that it would be nice to run up and down the slopes to pick flowers with Annette, but he did not think about it for long. There was so much else to be happy about. Besides, if he had not been lame he would never have had his bear crutches, nor would he have been sitting in the cart with his arms around the bull calf.

The path turned a hairpin bend around the roots of

a great pine tree, and as they turned the corner they came in sight of their summer home—a little shut-up cow barn with one living room joined onto it, standing in the middle of a meadow of yellow flowers. Just behind it rose the last steep slope of the rest of the mountain.

It seemed very welcoming, this hut, as though it was longing to be opened up and lived in again. The cows moved a little faster at the sight of it, and their lazy bells pealed out merrily.

A fountain splashed into a wooden trough outside the chalet, and the thirsty cattle plunged their heads into it and enjoyed a long, noisy drink. Dani and the calf tumbled out of the cart and drank, too. Then they all gathered around the door while Monsieur Burnier turned the key in the lock and went in.

The hut was damp and cold after being buried in snow all winter, but they had brought logs and provisions in the mule cart and soon they had lit a fire. As Annette flung back the shutters, the sun came streaming in, showing up the dust everywhere.

Around went Annette with a broom and duster, and Dani came hopping behind like a cheerful grasshopper. Monsieur Burnier vanished up a ladder into the loft to bring down armfuls of musty hay for the cows' bedding. Then it was milking time and the cattle wandered in one by one. After that it was suppertime, and Monsieur Burnier and Annette sat on stools at the table while Dani sat on a rug on the floor because the condition of his legs made stools uncomfortable for him. They ate bread, smoked sausage, and cheese and drank hot coffee out of enormous wooden bowls. It was a lovely meal.

When he had finished his last mouthful Dani struggled to his feet and held up his arms to his father.

"Do you want to go to bed now?" asked Monsieur Burnier, picking him up.

"No," replied Dani firmly, "I want you to carry me to the top of the mountain!"

Monsieur Burnier looked horrified. The top of the mountain was a good twenty-five minutes steep climb, and Dani was a heavy child. But he always found it impossible to refuse his little son anything, so he burst into a hearty roar of laughter at his own foolishness and started off with Dani on his shoulder. Dani drummed his heels against his father's chest while Annette clung to his coat-tail.

The mountaintop was covered with rare, beautiful flowers, and Annette ran among them while Monsieur Burnier strode on, too out of breath to speak. Only when they at last reached the top did he put Dani down, and then they all sat looking about them, thinking their own thoughts.

Everywhere they looked, rosy snow peaks rose upward. The sun was setting, and while twilight had fallen on the valleys below, the high mountains caught the last rays of the sun and were bathed in a bright pink glow. An English child might have thought that the Alps were on fire, but Dani, who was used to the sight, just sighed contentedly. As they sat watching, the sun sank a little lower until the very tips still burned crimson. Then the glow faded altogether and there was nothing to be seen at all but cold, ice-blue mountains with the stars coming out behind them. Soon the moon would rise and then the peaks would turn to dazzling silver.

It was nice to get back to the chalet and see the firelight flickering in the window, and to gather around the blazing logs and shut out the night. The door into the stable was open, and the calf came straying in and sat down on the floor by Dani, with its long legs crumpled up beneath it.

"I want to sleep with the calf," announced Dani in his firmest voice.

"No, Dani," said Annette quickly, "you will catch fleas."

"But if Napoleon had fleas I should have caught them already in the cart," reasoned Dani. "Please, Papa, I want very badly to sleep with Napoleon!"

Monsieur Burnier remarked that he thought it could be managed for a treat. So he rigged up a hay mattress covered with a sack, and Dani was tucked up on it under the rug while Napoleon happily lay on a heap of straw beside him. Annette slept in the one and only bed, and Monsieur Burnier went off and made himself comfortable in the hayloft.

12

Annette's Revenge

Lucien did not go up the mountain with his cows, for the Morels only had four cows, which they farmed out with another herd for the summer. So until hay making started in the fields around his home, Lucien had plenty of time after school. He went to visit the old man of the mountain nearly every day.

His horse was nearly finished, and it was a beautiful piece of work for a boy of Lucien's age. It was a larger model than he had ever tried before, with a flying mane and little hooves that hardly seemed to touch the ground. Lucien spent hours over it and studied every horse in the neighborhood so that he might make each muscle look perfect.

He still had plenty of time because the competition

was not going to be judged until the end of the hay-making holiday, but already the school children were beginning to make guesses about who would win.

Most of the boys thought it should be Michel, the milkman's son, who had carved two bears climbing up a pole. He had worked hard and it was a good piece of work, but they could easily have been mistaken for dogs or any other animals, thought Lucien, looking at them silently while the other children admired it loudly. Nobody could mistake his horse, thought Lucien. It was a horse and nothing but a horse.

Now, looking at Michel's bears, he knew he would win the prize. There was nothing as good as his entry.

He imagined himself walking up for the prize, and everyone looking at him in amazement and astonishment. Then they would all be interested and want to see his horse. And then perhaps they would like him better.

There was more discussion about the girls' entries. Annette was a skilled knitter. Grandmother had taught her when she didn't go to school. She had sat on her small stool keeping an eye on Dani and clicking away at her needles, with Grandmother sitting in her armchair ready to help her when she needed it.

Annette was entering a dark blue sweater she had knitted for Dani to wear on Sundays and festival days, with alpine flowers knitted in bright colors around the neck and waist. She had not finished it yet, but it was coming on nicely, and everybody praised it as she sat working away in the playground.

"I think you are sure to get the prize, Annette," said several of her friends. "It is harder to do a pattern like that than to make lace like Marcelle. Everyone says so."

Annette was hopeful, too. She wanted so badly to win that prize. It would make up a little for getting such bad marks in math. And how pleased and proud Grandmother, Papa, and Dani would be!

However, unlike Lucien, she had very little time, for her after-school hours were always busy. And now the hay-making holidays had begun, and all the children worked in the fields from dawn to dusk, side by side with the adults.

A great deal of friendly arranging had to be done at hay-making time. A neighbor who had grown-up sons to help on his farm went up to the high pastures to look after the Burnier cows, while Monsieur Burnier came down to cut the hay on his own slopes. After he had finished, he always went over and cut the hay in the little meadow that belonged to the Morels, because Madame Morel was a widow and Lucien was not yet old enough to swing a scythe.

There were no tractors or mowers on those steep mountain slopes, only great sweeping scythes that mowed the grass in curved bundles all up and down the field. Behind the man with the scythe came the women and children with wooden rakes, pulling the bundles into tidy heaps. Even the tiny children had tiny rakes, for as soon as a child could walk steadily on his legs he had to help with the hay making.

Papa and Annette had to work hard, for they had a large, sloping pasture and could not afford to pay anyone to help them. They got up at sunrise each morning in the cool, clear dawn to start their work. Later on in the day Grandmother and Dani joined them—Grandmother working slowly and painfully, and Dani doing no work at all because he couldn't manage a rake and a crutch at the same time. Instead he jumped like a kangaroo among the bundles of cut hay or buried himself under the large piles, and when he was tired out he lay flat on his back in the sun and fell asleep.

Monsieur Burnier cut his own meadow first and then went off to cut the Morels' field, leaving his family to gather in his own bundles of hay. Madame Morel had been rather worried this year that Monsieur Burnier would not want to help her because of Lucien causing Dani's accident. But she need not have worried, for she woke one morning and from her window she saw him hard at work, his brown body stripped to the waist, swinging the scythe. He was not the sort of man to take revenge.

"Hurry, Lucien," she called, "Monsieur Burnier is already mowing in the meadow. Run out and start raking in the hay."

Lucien shuffled off to the field feeling rather embarrassed. He said good morning to Monsieur Burnier, with his eyes fixed on the ground. He hated having to work with the man he had wronged, and kept as far away as possible. Monsieur Burnier had no wish to talk to him either. It was one thing to mow a neighbor's meadow, but quite another to chat with the boy who had injured his little son.

Annette arrived at midday with her father's lunch wrapped up in a cloth. She took no notice of Lucien, and when he saw her coming he slunk away into the house.

It took Monsieur Burnier three days to mow the Morel meadow, and the third day was the last day of the holidays. Lucien and his mother and sister were working hard to clear the field before Lucien went back to school. They were all in the meadow when Annette appeared, as usual, with her father's dinner. She was in a hurry, for the next day the children had to turn in their entries for the handwork competition, and Annette still had to put the finishing touches to her sweater.

"I do wonder if I shall get that prize," said Annette to herself. "I want it so much. But even if I don't, Dani will look sweet in the sweater."

The meadow lay at the back of the house, and on her way home Annette passed by the front. It was a very hot day, and Annette was thirsty. The door leading from the little balcony into the kitchen stood invitingly open.

"I will go in and have a drink from the tap," thought Annette, climbing the balcony steps. And indeed there was no harm in that. Before the accident Annette had run in and out of the Morel kitchen as though it was her own.

When she reached the top of the steps she suddenly stopped dead and stood quite still, staring and staring.

There was a little table set against the outer side of

the balcony with some carving tools and chips of wood on it. Amidst the chips was the figure of a little horse at full gallop, with waving mane and delicate hooves.

Annette stood for five whole minutes gazing at the little creature. Of course she realized that it was Lucien's entry for the handwork competition, and the deceitful boy had never even told anyone that he was entering, or that he knew how to carve at all.

It was almost perfect, even Annette's jealous eyes could see that. If he turned it in, he would win the prize easily. No one else's entry would be nearly as good. And when he won the prize, everybody would begin to admire his work and perhaps they would begin to like him for it. Perhaps they would even begin to forget that he had injured Dani.

And if Lucien won the prize, he would be happy. He would walk up to receive it with his head in the air, and to see Lucien looking happy would be more than Annette could bear. Why should he be happy? He deserved never to be happy again. He would not be happy if she could help it. She felt she had arrived just at the right time.

The table stood on the level with the balcony railings, and a gust of wind fluttered the shavings of wood. A stronger gust of wind could easily blow the light little model over. No one would ever suspect anything else when they found the little horse smashed and trampled in the mud below.

Annette put out her hand and pushed it over. It fell onto the stones with a little crack, and Annette bounded down the steps and stamped on it. Anyone could accidentally tread on something that had blown over the balcony railing.

So Lucien's horse lay in splinters among the cobblestones, and Annette walked slowly home.

But somehow the brightness had gone out of the day, and the world no longer looked quite as beautiful as before.

It was not long before she came in sight of her own chalet, and as she turned the corner, Dani saw her and gave a loud welcoming shout. Something very, very exciting had happened, and if he had been able to he would have raced to meet her. But, being on crutches, he hobbled up the hill as fast as he possibly could.

"'Nette, 'Nette," shouted Dani, his eyes shining, "I think there's been some fairies in the woodpile. I made a little house down by the logs and I found a tiny little elephant with a long trunk, and then I looked again and I found a camel with a hump, and a rabbit with long ears, and cows and goats and tigers and a giraffe with ever such a long neck. Oh, 'Nette, come and look at them. They are so beautiful, and no one but the fairies could have put them down beside the woodpile, could they?"

"I don't know," answered Annette, and her voice sounded quite cross. Dani looked up at her in astonishment. She didn't seem at all pleased about his news, and it was almost the most wonderful thing that had happened to him since he had found Klaus in his slipper on Christmas morning.

However, when she saw them she was sure to be pleased. She didn't yet know how beautiful they were. He hopped bravely along, rather out of breath because Annette was walking faster than she usually did when he was beside her.

He dragged her to the woodpile and dived behind it, reappearing with the procession of carved animals arranged on a flat log. He looked anxiously at her, but to his great disappointment there was no sign of surprise or pleasure in her face.

"I expect some other child dropped them, Dani," she said crossly, "and anyhow it's nothing to make such a fuss about. They are not all that wonderful. And you're too big to believe in fairies."

She turned away and went up the steps, hating herself. She had been unkind to Dani and spoiled all his happiness. How could she have spoken to him like that? What had happened to her?

But deep down inside she knew quite well what had happened to her. She had done a mean, deceitful thing, and her heart was heavy and dark at the thought of it. All the light and joy seemed to have gone out of life.

And now she could never get rid of it or undo it. She ran upstairs to her bedroom and, flinging herself on the bed, she burst into tears.

13

The Old Man's Story

Lucien ran home from the fields with a light heart that evening. He had worked hard, and his body was tired, but his little horse was waiting for him. Tomorrow he would carry it to school and everyone would know that he could carve.

Up the steps he bounded, and then stopped dead. His horse was gone. Only the tools and the wood chips lay on the table.

Perhaps his mother, who had come home earlier, had taken it in. He hurled himself into the house.

"Mother! Mother," he cried, "where have you put my little horse?"

His mother looked up from the soup pot. "I haven't seen it," she replied. "You must have put it somewhere yourself."

Lucien began to get seriously alarmed.

"I haven't," he answered. "I left it on the table, I *know* I did. Oh, Mother, *where* can it be? Do help me find it!"

His mother followed him at once. She was just as keen on Lucien winning the prize as he was himself, and together they hunted high and low. Then Madame Morel had an idea.

"Perhaps it has fallen over the railing, Lucien," she said. "Go and search for it down below."

So Lucien went down and searched. He did not need to search for long. He found it all too quickly— the muddy, scattered splinters of wood that had once been his horse.

He gathered them up in his hand and took them to his mother. Her cry of disappointment brought Marie running out, and both of them stood gazing in dismay.

"It must have been the cat," said Marie at last. "I am sorry, Lucien. Haven't you anything else you could take?"

His mother said nothing except "Oh, Lucien!" But the voice in which she said it meant quite a lot.

Lucien said nothing at all. He just went indoors and looked at the clock on the wall.

"I'm going up the mountain," he said in a voice that tried hard to be steady. "I won't be home for supper."

He ran down the balcony steps and up through the hay field where the bundles of hay looked like waves in a green sea. His mother watched him with a troubled face until he disappeared into the forest. Then she went back and wept a few tears into the soup pot.

"Everything goes wrong for that boy," she murmured sadly. "Will he ever succeed in anything?"

Lucien trudged through the forest, seeing nothing. He took no notice of the little grey squirrels that leapt from branch to branch. He could think of nothing at all but his lost prize and his bitter disappointment—how someone else would get the honor that he deserved, and he would continue to be disliked and despised. He would never get another chance to show them how good he was at carving. No one would be interested unless he won that prize.

"I wish I could go away," he thought to himself, "and start all over again where nobody knew me, or knew what I'd done. If I could go and live in another valley, I shouldn't feel afraid of everybody like I do here."

His eyes rested on the Pass that ran between two opposite mountain peaks and led to the big town in the next valley where Marie worked. The sight of that Pass always fascinated him. It seemed like a road leading into another world, away from all that was safe and familiar. Twice he had crossed the Pass himself, in summer, when the sun was shining and the ground was covered with flowers. Now, gazing at it, it suddenly seemed like a door of escape from some prison.

Lucien saw the old man as he left the wood, long before the old man saw him. He was sitting at his front door, his chin resting on his hands, gazing at the mountains on the other side of the valley. He didn't look up until Lucien was quite close to him.

"Ah," said the old man in his deep, mumbling voice, "it's you again. Well, how goes the carving, and when are you going to win that prize?"

"I am not going to win the prize," replied Lucien sullenly. "My horse is smashed to pieces. I think the cat knocked it over the railing, and someone trampled on it."

"I am so sorry," said the old man gently. "But surely you can enter something else. What about that chamois you carved? That was a good piece of work for a boy."

Lucien kicked savagely at the stones on the path. "I did it without proper tools," he muttered, "and they would think it was my best work. No, if I cannot enter my little horse, I will enter nothing."

"But does it matter what they think?" inquired the old man.

"Yes," muttered Lucien again.

"Why?"

Lucien stared at the ground. What could he answer to that? But the old man was his friend, almost the only friend he had. Maybe he had better try to speak the truth.

"It matters very much," he mumbled, "because they all hate me and think I'm stupid and bad. If I won a prize, and they saw I could carve better than any other boy in the valley, they might like me better."

"They wouldn't," he said simply. "Your skill can never buy you love. It may win you admiration and envy, but never love. If that was what you were after, you have wasted your time."

Lucien continued to stare at the ground. Then suddenly he looked up into the old man's face, his eyes brimming with tears.

"Then it is all no good," he whispered. "There seems no way to start again and to make them like me. I suppose they just never will."

"If you want them to like you," replied the old man steadily, "you must make yourself fit to be liked. And you must use your skill in loving and serving them. It will not happen all at once. It may even take years, but you must keep trying."

Lucien stared up at the old man. He wondered why this strange old man, who seemed to know so much about the way of love, should shut himself away up here in the mountains and cut himself off from everybody.

The old man seemed to guess what Lucien was thinking.

"You wonder why I should talk of loving and serving other people, don't you?" he asked. "You are right to wonder such a thing. It is a long story, too."

"Well," admitted Lucien, "I was thinking that it must be difficult to love and serve people when you live alone up here and never speak to anyone but me."

The old man sat silent for some moments, looking out over the mountain peaks, then said, "I will tell you my story, but remember, it is a secret. I have never told it to another living soul. But you have trusted me, and I will trust you, too."

Lucien blushed. Those were good words. Even his disappointment about the prize seemed to matter less. It was better to be trusted than to win prizes.

"I will start at the beginning," said the old man simply. "I was an only child, and there was nothing in the world my father would not give me. If ever a child was spoiled, I was.

"I was a clever boy, and when I grew up I had a good job in a bank. I worked very hard and did well. I fell in love with a girl and married her. God gave us two little sons, and for the first few years of our life together I believe I was a good husband and a good father.

"But I made some bad friends, who invited me to their homes. They were interested in gambling and they drank a lot of alcohol. I admired them and began to copy their ways. Slowly I began to spend more and more money on strong drink and gambling.

"I don't need to tell you much about those years. I was at home less and less, and often came home drunk in the evenings. My little boys grew to dislike me and fear me. My wife was a good woman, and she prayed for me and begged me to stop drinking, but I just couldn't give it up.

"We began to lose all our money, and people were starting to talk about me and my bad ways. The bank manager warned me twice, but the third time, when I was found drunk in the streets, he sacked me. That day I went home sober and told my wife I had lost my job. She simply replied, 'Then I shall have to go out and work. We can't fail our boys.'

"I tried to find another job, but people knew about me and no one would employ me. I tried to earn money by gambling, but I never had any luck. I lost the little money I had.

"My wife went out to work every day, as well as looking after the house and our two boys, but she could not earn enough to keep us all. One day she came and told me we owed money to people, and we could not pay them.

"I was desperate for money to pay our debts and to buy myself more drink. I had not had a good job in the bank for nothing. I knew its ways inside and out, so I decided to commit a robbery.

"My clever plan worked, but it was not quite clever enough and I was caught. As I could pay nothing back to the bank, I was sent to prison for a very long time.

"My wife became very ill. She was working too hard, and ate hardly anything so that our boys would have enough food. Three times she came to prison to visit me, looking pale and worn out. Then my elder boy wrote to tell me that she was too ill to come. A few weeks later a policeman took me to her bedside to say good-bye to her. She was dying. They said she died from tuberculosis, but I knew she died of a broken heart, and I had killed her.

"I remember little about the months that followed. I felt numb and lost. I had only one comfort. All my life I had loved woodcarving, and in my spare hours in the common room in prison they let me have my tools and whittle away at bits of wood. I grew more and more skillful, and a kind prison warden used to take my work and sell it in the town. I earned a little money in that way and saved it up. One day I hoped to have enough to start again.

"The day came sooner than I expected. I was called to the governor and told that because I had been well behaved, they were letting me out early. I would soon be a free man again.

"I wandered back to the prisoners' common room, hardly knowing whether to be pleased or sorry. I supposed I should be glad to leave prison, but where should I go, and how could I start life again? One thing I was sure about: my boys should never see me again or know where I was. They had been adopted by their grandparents, and I knew they were growing up into fine, intelligent boys with good futures ahead of them. I didn't want them to be connected with my bad name. To them I would be as though I was dead.

"When the day of my release came, I walked out with my little sum of money in my pocket and took the first train up into the mountains.

"I got out at this village because I saw a man in difficulty with his herd of cows who were trying to push through a broken fence. I helped him get them back into the road and then asked him if he could give me work.

"He did not need me, but pointed to a chalet halfway up the mountain. Up there, he told me, was a peasant whose son had gone down to the lake towns to learn a trade. He badly needed someone to take the place of his son.

"I shall never forget that day! I found the chalet, and the man himself was chopping wood outside when I arrived. I went and stood in front of him. I was tired and hungry and sick at heart, and wasted no time in asking him if he had a job for me.

"He looked me up and down. His face was good and his eyes were kind.

"'You are not from our village,' he said. 'Where have you come from, and who are you?'

"I come from Geneva."

"'What is your work?'

"'I have none.'

"'But what have you been doing up to now?'

I tried to think up some good lie, but the man looked at me so straight, and his face was so honest, that I knew I had to tell him the truth. I wanted him to know me for what I was, or else not to know me at all.

"'I have just come out of prison,' I said simply.

"'Why were you in prison?'

"'For stealing money.'

"'How do I know that you will not steal my money?'

"'Because I want to start again, and I am asking you to trust me. If you do not trust me, I will go away.'

"He looked me up and down. Then he held out his hand to me, and I sat down on the bench beside him and wept.

"I worked hard for that man for five years. I made friends with no one and took no rest. My only joy was to work for the man I loved and who had received me when everyone else had rejected me. I often wondered why he did it, until one night I heard him talking to his son, who was home from town for the weekend.

" 'Father,' said the boy, 'why did you take in that prisoner without knowing anything about him? Surely it was a very unwise thing to do.'

" 'My son,' answered the man, 'Christ received everyone, whether they were good or bad, and we are his followers. We must do the same.'

"In the summer we took the cows up the mountain and lived in this chalet where I live now. And the peace of the mountain seemed to enter into me and heal me. Slowly I, too, began to believe in the love and mercy of God.

"But after four years my master began to grow weak and ill. He visited the doctor, but nothing could be done for him. I cared for him for a year and his son often came to see him, but at last he died and I was left alone. The night before he died, he spoke to me, as my wife had done, about the love and mercy of God and how He can forgive us for what we have done wrong.

"So I lost my only friend, although his son was very good to me. He was a rich man by now. He sold the cows and gave me this chalet for my own. I bought a goat and a few hens, collected my few possessions, and came here. I have lived here ever since.

"I have only one friend—the shopkeeper in town who sells my carvings. He sometimes gives me news of my sons. They have grown up into good men and they have done well. One is a doctor and one is a businessman. They do not know that I am alive, and it is better like that. I have nothing that I could give them, and my name would only disgrace them.

"Because I now believe in God, and His love and

mercy, I want to make things right. I cannot give back the money I stole from the bank, but I have worked hard and saved nearly as much money as I stole. When I have saved the whole amount, I will find some person or good cause that really needs it. In that way I shall pay back all I owe and I will feel I have put things right.

"You tell me there is no way to start again, but you are wrong. I have done far, far worse things than you have ever done, and suffered for it. But I believe that God has forgiven me, and I am spending my days working to give back what I owe and trying to become what God meant me to be. It is all I can do. It is all anyone can do. The past we must leave to God."

The goat had come up and rested its brown head on the old man's knee. Now it butted him to remind him that it was milking time. Lucien got up to go.

He walked home slowly. "I am spending my days working to restore what I owe . . . trying to become what God meant me to be." He thought about it a lot—so much so that the matter of the prize seemed quite small, and he found that he had stopped minding so much. He couldn't restore Dani's leg, but one day he might get the chance to do something great for him. As for the second part, he could at least try to be a nicer boy. There was his mother, for a start. She was miserable because his carving was broken. Well, he would be brave and show her he didn't mind, and then she would be happy again.

As he left the wood he could see the orange lights in his chalet windows shining out warm and welcoming. He hurried home and ran lightly up the chalet steps and kissed his mother, who was standing on the balcony watching for him.

"I'm hungry, Mother," he said brightly. "Have you saved my supper?"

Over the top of his soup bowl he smiled at her, and the sadness left her eyes as she smiled back.

14

The Handwork Competition

The sun woke Dani early next morning, and he lay for a few minutes trying to remember what important thing was going to happen that day. It soon came back to him, and he sat up in bed and shouted for Annette.

"'Nette," he called, "come quick! I'm coming to see you get the prize! Bring me my best black velvet suit and my embroidered braces and my waistcoat. *Quick!*"

Annette pretended not to hear until he had said it four times. Then she sat up.

"Be quiet, Dani," she called back rather crossly. "I don't suppose I shall get that prize at all, and anyhow it's much too early to get dressed. Papa's only just got up."

Dani sighed and lay down again, but he was too excited to stop talking. He pulled Klaus into bed with him and began whispering into one of her silky white ears.

"I shall go in the cart, Klaus," he murmured, "and I shall see all the things the children have made. But Annette's is the best, and I shall see her get a lovely prize, and I'll clap as loud as I can. And I shall wear my best braces."

Klaus yawned. So did Dani. After all, it was very early in the morning. When Annette came down later, she found them curled up into two little balls, fast asleep in the sun.

One and a half hours later they were off, with Dani dressed in his best clothes. Papa pulled the cart and Annette walked beside him, feeling dull and sad and rather cross.

What could be making Annette so miserable on such a morning? The sun was shining, the river was glistening, and Annette was going to win a prize. There was everything to make them happy, and anyhow Dani never felt sad or cross except when he had a pain in his leg.

"Have you got a tummy ache, 'Nette?" asked Dani suddenly.

"Of course I haven't, Dani," answered Annette sharply. "Why should I have a tummy ache?"

"I just thought you might," replied Dani. "Oh, 'Nette, look. There's a blue butterfly sitting on my shoe."

But Annette did not even turn around to look at the blue butterfly. She walked on, staring at the ground.

Whatever could be the matter with Annette?

Already the schoolroom was filling when they arrived. The desks had been stacked on one side and the children's work was laid out on long tables knitting, embroidery, lace, and crochet work—making a very pretty show. Parents walked around admiringly while children jostled and nudged each other, pointing and chattering like magpies.

Pierre, the postman's son, was standing by the wood-carving table, close to his own piece of work: a wooden inkstand with a bear standing over the inkwell. It was quite a good piece of work for a child of his age. Pierre, who was a nice boy, blushed a little and looked the other way as his friends slapped him on the back and congratulated him. Still, he was pleased with that little bear himself, and he looked up and smiled proudly at his mother, who was coming toward him across the room.

Lucien was there, too, wandering around by himself as usual, for his mother had not finished getting the hay in and had not come down. He stared gloomily at the inkstand and compared the heavy-looking bear with his own sprightly galloping horse. If only that accident had not happened, the children would have been standing around him instead of round Pierre. He felt a great angry stab of jealousy for Pierre, who was clever and good-looking and good at games, and who now was going to win the prize that belonged to Lucien. He drifted away into a corner by himself and stared gloomily at the crowd.

Annette, surrounded by a group of chattering friends, was strangely silent. Some thought she would get the prize; others thought Jeanne might win. There was much guessing and running to and fro, and much putting together of heads, some saying one thing and some another. Only Annette, usually so bright and talkative, said nothing.

Dani, his hand clasped tightly in his father's, hopped around inspecting everything, and everyone made way for him and gave him a kind word as he passed. Then, having seen all he wanted to see, he went to stand at the end of the long table close to Annette's entry so that he might be right on the spot when the prizewinner was announced.

The door opened and a sudden hush fell on the chattering crowd. The man from the town by the lake had arrived to judge the work. The children and parents stood quietly against the walls as the tall man walked slowly around, picking up and examining first one thing and then another. He praised a great many of the entries and spoke kindly about all of them. He had come prepared to see a good exhibition, he said, and he was not disappointed. He looked through the children's exercise books, piled on a table at the far end of the room, and talked about their work. He was a kind, patient man, but very slow. All that the children wanted to know was *who* was going to get the prize.

He was going to make up his mind about the girls first. He walked over to Marcelle's lace and examined it carefully, then went back to Annette's knitted sweater and turned it over in his hands. The room was so silent you could have heard a pin drop.

Then suddenly the silence was broken.

"My sister made that," said a clear, distinct child's voice.

The big man jumped and peered over the end of the table. He saw a small brown face with round blue eyes lifted to his, alight with hope and eagerness.

"Then your sister is a very clever girl," replied the big man gravely, and as he spoke he noticed the crutches.

"I think it's the very best of all, don't you?" went on Dani earnestly, not noticing at all that everyone in the room was listening to him. All he knew was that he wanted Annette to win.

The big man had not quite made up his mind when Dani first spoke, but now he suddenly felt quite certain.

"Yes, I do. I think it's the very best," answered the big man, and Dani immediately turned round on his crutches and faced his sister, who was blushing deeply at his bad behaviour.

"You've got the prize, 'Nette," called out Dani, and everybody burst out laughing and started clapping. And so, in this unusual and unexpected fashion, the prizewinner for the girls was announced.

Pierre won the boys' prize. It was announced properly after a suitable speech to which none of the children listened. Then there was tea and rolls and gingerbread and macaroons, and then Pierre went home with a crowd of admiring friends, who all bought chocolate sticks for him for winning.

Lucien went down to the village alone to collect the bread, and when he came back past the school, the playground was deserted and the children had all gone home. He climbed the hill slowly, but it was not the weight of the bread basket on his back that bowed his shoulders and made him walk with his eyes on the ground.

Lucien was very unhappy. Why was it that one day it seemed easy to be brave and cheerful, and the next day it seemed impossible to be anything but angry and jealous? Yesterday, on the way home from visiting the old man, he had thought that he wouldn't mind seeing Pierre win the prize. But today he hated Pierre. The old man had talked about trying to become what God meant you to be, but somehow, however hard you tried, it seemed impossible to change yourself for long.

And yet the old man had become different, and Lucien found himself wondering how. The old man had talked about God. Perhaps God could make nasty people nice if they asked Him. Lucien felt he didn't know very much about God. Anyhow, God was probably very angry with him for being so wicked to Dani.

But could God really love him much? Surely God wouldn't forgive something so bad in a hurry. And even if He did, nobody else would. His unhappiness came over him again, and he gave a great sniff and kicked angrily at the stones on the path.

He was passing the corner where the path divided, not far from Annette's chalet, and as he branched off toward his home he suddenly heard a little child singing. He turned to look.

Dani and Klaus were sitting on a hollowed-out pile of new hay, like two birds in a nest, and Dani's bright head was bent low over something. His crutches lay on the ground beside him.

Because he was feeling so lonely, Lucien drew a step nearer and stood watching. Suddenly his cheeks flushed with pleasure and he drew a sharp little breath. Dani had dug out a sort of cave in the wall of his hay nest, and inside it were grouped all the little wooden animals that Lucien had carved with such care.

"So she *did* give them to him," thought Lucien to himself with a little thrill of happiness. "And he does like them!" Then, aloud, he said, "What are you playing at, Dani?"

Dani jumped and looked up, and saw the boy who had tried to kill his kitten. His first reaction was to seize Klaus around the middle tightly and say, "Go away, you horrid boy!"

But as he said it, he, although he was only five years old, could not help noticing that Lucien looked very unhappy, and unhappiness was a thing that his friendly little heart could not bear. So, still holding the struggling Klaus very tightly, he added after a moment's pause, "I'm playing with my fairy Noah animals, but 'Nette said I mustn't talk to you."

"I wouldn't hurt you," answered Lucien very gently. "And I'm sorry about your leg. That's why I made those animals for you."

"You didn't make them," answered Dani cheerfully. "I found them behind the woodpile. The fairies put them there."

Lucien was just about to answer when Annette's voice came sharp and shrill from the door of the chalet.

"Dani," she shouted, "come in at once. Supper's ready."

Lucien turned away. "So she didn't tell him," he thought rather bitterly. Still, it was nice to know that Dani loved them and played with them. One day he might get the chance to explain, and then perhaps he and Dani would be friends. He climbed the path between the hay fields feeling a bit more cheerful.

Dani hopped into the kitchen and climbed into his seat, his nose twitching joyfully like a rabbit's at the smell of Grandmother's potato soup.

"'Nette," began Dani, "Lucien said that he made my fairy Noah animals, but he didn't, did he? The fairies put them behind the woodpile, didn't they? He wasn't speaking the truth, was he?"

"I've told you not to talk to Lucien, Dani," said Annette crossly. "He'll only hurt you again. He's a horrid boy."

"Yes," answered Dani, "and I only talked to him a teeny, weeny bit. But he didn't, did he, 'Nette? Tell me!"

Annette hesitated. She was a truthful child, and she did not want to tell a lie. But if Dani knew, he would be so grateful that he would forgive Lucien at once, and go and thank him. And there was no telling where it would all end. They would become friends in a few minutes. It was hard enough as it was to make Dani unfriendly with anybody, but if he knew about the animals it would be quite impossible.

"You know you found them in the woodpile," she replied, looking away, "so how could he have made them? Don't be silly, Dani."

"He said he did," answered Dani, "but I know he didn't. It must have been the fairies, mustn't it, 'Nette?"

"Oh, I don't know, Dani," replied poor Annette wearily. "How you do chatter! Eat up your soup quickly. It will be all cold."

Dani obediently buried his nose in his bowl, but Grandmother, whose dim old eyes saw more than most people's, looked very hard at Annette. She, too, had heard and wondered at the story of the animals in the woodpile.

Annette, knowing that Grandmother was looking hard at her, went very red. Going over to the stove, she pretended to help herself to more soup. But she only took a little, for somehow she wasn't a bit hungry. The day she had looked forward to for so long was all spoiled. She had got the prize she wanted so badly, but it hadn't made her a bit happy. In fact, she was really miserable.

She washed up the supper things in silence, tucked up, and kissed a warm, sleepy Dani. Then she slipped out alone into the summer evening. She usually loved being out alone on summer evenings to do just as she pleased—just her and the still blue mountains.

But tonight it was different. Nothing pleased her, and she could think of nothing but that smashed little horse lying trampled on the ground, and of the light that had died in Dani's face when she had spoken so crossly to him.

"Perhaps I shall never like being alone again," thought poor Annette, and she turned back toward home. "I wish I could tell someone! It wouldn't be so bad then. I wish Mummy was still alive. Oh, I wish, I wish, I *wish* I hadn't done it!"

15

Christmas Again—and Gingerbread Bears

Autumn came, and the cows returned from the high pastures. Dani was growing taller every day, and by October the village cobbler had to make him a new pair of boots. He went to the infant school, too, every day, and Monsieur Burnier paid two big boys one franc each a week to pull him home in the cart.

And now Christmas had come around again. The snow lay over a foot deep on the chalet roofs, and Papa had to dig a path from the front door to the main sled track. The little stream was silent and frozen, and icicles hung like bright swords from the rocks. Annette and Dani went to school on the sled every morning by starlight, but came home in the sunshine under a deep blue sky, the snow sparkling like jewels.

Christmas was a very special time to Dani, for all the great events of his life had happened at Christmas. His mother had died on Christmas Eve, and though Dani had never known his mother, he sensed a certain gentle sadness in his father's face and felt a special tenderness toward him and Annette. Dani himself had had all the mothering he needed from Grandmother and Annette, and the only time he ever thought about his mother was when Grandmother read about heaven in the Bible. Then he would gaze up into her photograph on the wall, and think that when his time came to go to heaven it would be nice to see her kind face, so like Annette's, looking out for him and smiling to welcome him.

It was his own birthday, too, and this year he was six. He had thought for a long time about being six, and he expected to wake up quite a new child on the morning of Christmas Eve. So it was rather disappointing to find, as he lay in the warm, shuttered darkness, that he really felt no bigger or stronger or more important than before. Then he remembered that he was going to see the Christmas tree in the church, and Grandmother had made a special cake for his birthday, and after that there was no room for disappointed thoughts any longer.

Of course, according to Dani, Christmas was Klaus's birthday, too. It wasn't really Klaus's birthday because Klaus must have been at least a fortnight old when she crept into Dani's slipper, but Dani had never thought of that.

Best of all, it was the birthday of the Lord Jesus,

and although Dani did not talk about it very much, he thought about it a lot. It made him strangely happy to know that he shared the birthday of the perfect child.

"What could I give to the little Lord Jesus for a birthday present?" he had asked, resting his elbows on Grandmother's knee and looking up into her face.

"You can give your own self to Him," Grandmother had answered, pausing a moment in her knitting. "And you can ask Him to make you very loving and obedient. That will please Him better than anything."

So throughout Christmas, Dani tried to be loving and obedient in order to please the child whose birthday he shared, and his love just overflowed to everyone. He tidied Grandmother's workbox and wiped the dishes for Annette. In the afternoon he went out to the shed and visited the cows in turn, wishing Happy Christmas into their silky ears. And at the end of the day, when he said his prayers, he whispered, "I hope I am giving you a happy birthday, little Lord Jesus."

So Dani had a perfect birthday, and when evening came and it was time to wrap up warmly and go down to the church, his happiness was complete.

To begin with, there was the ride on the sled between Papa and Annette, with the cold air making his nose feel as though it wasn't there. It was almost full moon, and the white mountains looked quite silvery. All the trees in the forest were weighed down with snow, and the lower branches trembled as they rushed past. Annette held him tightly around the middle, which made him feel very warm and safe.

Out of the wood, over the bumpy little bridge and down across the last field with a cold rush, there was the little church with the rosy light of hundreds of candles streaming from the windows and door, and the villagers greeting each other in the porch. Dani was carried up the aisle in Papa's arms and placed on the front bench with the other children from the infant school—thirty little rosy-faced children in woolly hoods gazing in wonder at the tree. Only three days ago it had been weighed down with snow in the cold forest near Dani's house. Now it was decorated and sparkling, covered with oranges, chocolate sticks, and shining gingerbread bears.

Dani was glad he was sitting in front, partly because he could see the tree, and partly because he could see his picture. It hung behind the pulpit—a great big picture of the Good Samaritan. It was hung in a wooden frame and had been drawn by a famous Swiss artist. Dani loved the kind face of the Good Samaritan, and he loved the little donkey. But best of all he loved the big St. Bernard dog that trotted along beside them. It was exactly like Rudolf, the St. Bernard dog that pulled the milk cart around the market square. He actually belonged to the milkman, but all the little children in the village thought he belonged to them. They climbed on his back and flung their fat, tight arms around his fluffy neck, and he licked them and patted them and was so patient with them, as though they were a crowd of naughty puppies. That was why every toddler in the church loved to come to church and see the picture of the Good Samaritan, with Rudolph trotting beside him.

The older children sang a carol first. Annette was singing it with the others, and her thoughts flew back to that Christmas night when she had first held Dani in her arms. How they had welcomed him and watched him. Yet no one but His mother had welcomed Baby Jesus. "They laid Him in a manger, because there was no room for them in the inn."

The carol finished, the older children went back to their seats and the infant school trotted to the front. Dani got left behind because crutches do not move as fast as sturdy legs, but they waited for him, and everyone in the audience smiled as he reached his place with a final hop and turned his happy face toward them.

Dani glanced up at the bright star on top of the Christmas tree and saw it reflected on the shining gingerbread bears below, and forgot what he was singing because he was wondering which particular bear was going to belong to him. There was one that looked as if it was laughing. The baker had accidentally given a little twist to its snout. Dani decided he would like that one.

As the children went back to their seats, the old pastor climbed into the pulpit. He had been pastor in that village for forty-five years and everybody loved him. His shoulders were bowed and his skin tanned, for he still climbed the mountain in all weather to visit his church members. His beard was so long and white that Dani got him mixed up in his mind with Father Christmas.

He looked down on the people he loved and knew so well. He was a very old man. This might be his last Christmas message. He prayed that he might speak words that would not be forgotten.

Annette listened rather dreamily to the story she knew so well, half thinking of other things, until the old man suddenly repeated the words that had haunted her every Christmas.

"There was no room for them—no room for *Him*!"

In the slow manner of some very old people, he repeated it three times, and each time Annette thought the words sounded sadder. How quickly she would have opened her door!

"And yet," went on the old man, "tonight the Savior is standing at closed doors. There are still hearts that have never made room for Him. This is what He says: 'Behold, I stand at the door, and knock: if any man hear my voice, and open the door, I will come in.'

"What will you do about Him this Christmas? Will you open the door, or will you leave Him standing outside? Will those sad words be said about you, 'There was no room for Him'?"

"I should like to ask Him to come in," thought Annette. "I wonder what it all means. The clergyman spoke about asking Him to come into our hearts. I wonder if I could ask Him into *my* heart."

Just for a moment Annette thought it rather a nice idea, and looked around to see whether other people thought it was, too. As she looked around, she suddenly noticed Lucien sitting on the other side of the church with his mother and sister.

As she caught sight of him she realized that she couldn't ask Jesus to come into her heart because her heart was full of hatred for Lucien. Jesus would not want to come into an angry, unforgiving heart. Either she would have to forgive and be kind, or else the Lord Jesus would have to stay outside.

She didn't want to forgive and be kind. Not yet.

There was something else, too. She had broken Lucien's carving and let him think it was the cat, and cheated him of his prize. If the Lord Jesus came into her heart, He would have something to say to her about that, and she didn't want to listen.

The sermon was over, but she had not heard much of it because she had been so busy with her thoughts. Dani nudged her to make her see that it was time for him to go up and get his gingerbread bear.

The church was full of a low murmur of conversation, and the little ones were pushing forward toward the tree. Monsieur Pilet, the woodcutter, was handing out bears. Dani gave his sleeve a firm tug and pointed to the bear at the top, which he wanted.

"Please, I want that one," he whispered, "that one up there. Please, I want it very badly!"

Because of the crutches, and because it was Christmas, Monsieur Pilet moved the ladders, moved the children, and moved the lower lights, and with great difficulty he climbed up and took hold of the bear that Dani wanted.

Dani was dragged home through the starlight and the snow with the bear he had specially chosen close to him. Every time he looked down at that merry curved snout he chuckled, as though he and his bear had some private Christmas joke between them that nobody else knew about.

16

Klaus Goes Missing

Christmas Day was over, and Dani was asleep with his flushed cheek lying on his arm. Papa was in the stable, and Annette and Grandmother sat one each side of the stove. Grandmother was knitting white woollen stockings for her grandchildren, and Annette was supposed to be patching her pinafore. Actually, her pinafore had slipped to the ground and she was simply staring in front of her with her head resting on her hands.

"Annette," said Grandmother suddenly, without looking up from her knitting, "have you had a happy Christmas?"

"Yes, thank you, Grandmother," replied Annette rather dully, because that's what she thought she ought to say. Then she added suddenly,

140

"Grandmother, what does it mean when it says that Jesus knocks at the door of our hearts?"

"It means," said Grandmother, laying down her knitting and giving Annette her whole attention, "that Jesus sees that your life is full of wrong things and dark thoughts. He came down and died on the cross so that He could be punished for all those wrong deeds and dark thoughts instead of you. Then He came back to life again so that He could come into your life and live in you, and turn out all those wrong thoughts, and put His good loving thoughts in you instead. It's like someone knocking at the door of a dirty, dark, dusty house and saying, 'If you will let me in I will take away the dust and the darkness and make it beautiful and bright.' But remember, Jesus never *pushes* His way in—He only asks if He may come in. That is what knocking means. You have to say, 'Yes, Lord Jesus, I need you and I want you to come and live in me.' That's what opening the door means."

Annette's eyes were fixed on Grandmother. There was a long, long pause.

Annette broke the silence.

"But Grandmother," she said, drawing her stool nearer and leaning against the old woman's knee, "if you hated someone, you could not ask Jesus to come in, could you?"

"If you hate someone," said Grandmother, "it just shows how badly you need to ask Him to come in. The darker the room, the more it needs the light."

"But I couldn't stop hating Lucien," said Annette softly, fingering her long plaits thoughtfully.

"No," said Grandmother. "You're quite right. None of us can stop ourselves thinking wrong thoughts, and it isn't much good trying. But Annette, when you come down in the morning and find this room dark with the shutters closed, do you say to yourself, 'I must chase away the darkness and the shadows first, and *then* I will open the shutters and let in the sun'? Do you waste time trying to get rid of the dark?"

"Of course not," said Annette.

"Then how do you get rid of the dark?"

"I pull back the shutters, of course, and then the light comes in!"

"But what happens to the dark?"

"I don't know. It just goes when the light comes!"

"That is just what happens when you ask the Lord Jesus to come in," said Grandmother. "He is love, and when love comes in, hatred and selfishness and unkindness will give way to it, just as the darkness gives way when you let in the sunshine. To try to chase it out alone would be like trying to chase the shadows out of a dark room. It would be a waste of time."

Annette did not answer. She only sat for a little time staring at the wall. Then she picked up her pinafore with a sigh and worked at it in silence. After a while she got up, kissed her grandmother good night very quietly, and went up to bed.

But she could not go to sleep for a long time. She lay in the dark, tossing and turning and wondering.

"It's quite true," she said to herself. "If I asked Him to come in, I should have to be friends with

Lucien, and I don't want to be. I suppose I should have to tell how I broke his carving, and I could never, *never* do that. I shall just have to try and forget about the knocking. And yet I feel so terribly miserable."

She did not know yet that the child who hears the Lord Jesus knocking, and shuts Him out, is also shutting out happiness. She thought she could forget all about it and find some other way of being happy. So she turned over her pillow, and made herself count the goats running to pasture until she fell asleep.

In her sleep she dreamed of a dark house with no welcome lights in the windows, and the door barred and bolted. Somebody came to it at night across the waste of snow, and she could see his footprints all the way. This visitor knocked at the door, slowly and patiently, but nobody came to open it. He felt for a handle, but there wasn't one. He went on knocking and knocking and knocking. He went on knocking until Annette woke up, but still nobody answered, and there were still no lights in the windows.

"Perhaps there's nobody there," thought Annette to herself in a half-asleep sort of way. But somehow she knew perfectly well that there was. They just didn't want to come to the door.

The sadness of the dream lingered with her, and she dressed and went down to breakfast feeling rather upset, only to find everything in a turmoil. Dani had lost Klaus, and was refusing to eat his breakfast until she was found.

"She always wakes me in the morning," explained Dani excitedly. "She comes and purrs at me. But this morning she wasn't there. She went out last night before I went to sleep, and she hasn't come back."

Dani was upset, and everyone tried to help him. Papa searched in the barns, Grandmother rummaged about in the kitchen, and Dani explored perfectly impossible places. Annette went upstairs and searched the bedrooms, but it was all in vain. Klaus was nowhere to be found. Papa had last seen her stalking toward the barn with her tail in the air, picking her way gingerly across the soft snow. No one had seen her since.

It was a miserable day. Dani was really upset at dinner, and between his sobs declared that he could not eat anything because Klaus was hungry. His tears trickled down into his soup and no one had any power to comfort him, although neither Papa nor Grandmother seemed particularly worried. "She will come back, Dani," said Papa quietly. "She's only hiding for today."

There was no sun either. Grey clouds hung low, hiding the mountains, and fresh, soft snow began to fall. At night it would harden into a crust, and next day would be dangerous for walking. Papa pulled on his cape and got out the big sleigh to haul in logs. Grandmother went to sleep in the armchair by the stove, and Dani came and leaned against Annette and looked up into her face.

"'Nette," he said pitifully, "I want to go to bed."

"Why, Dani?" asked Annette, astonished. "It's ever so early—only just beginning to get dark. And

144

you haven't had your supper!"

"But I want to go to bed, 'Nette," persisted Dani. "You see, I want it to be time to say my prayers."

Annette gave a little laugh. "You don't have to go to bed to say your prayers, Dani," she replied. "You could say them just as well now, and then have your supper and go to bed at the normal time."

But Dani shook his fair head. "No," he said, "I want them to be my proper prayers, in my night-gown. Please put me to bed, 'Nette."

"Oh, all right," answered Annette, beginning to unbutton his sweater. "But you know, Dani, it doesn't really make any difference being in your night-gown." And then she kissed him because his small face looked so terribly sad and his mouth dropped at the corners.

When he was safely buttoned into his white night-shirt, he knelt down and folded his hands and prayed for Klaus.

"Dear God," he prayed, "please bless Klaus. Please find her and bring her back to me quickly. Don't let her be cold or hungry or frightened. Show her the way home tonight. Please, please, dear God. Amen."

"Aren't you going to pray for anyone else?" protested Annette in a slightly shocked voice.

"No," replied Dani, getting up from his knees in a hurry, "not tonight. I don't want God to think of anyone but Klaus tonight!" And then, thinking that perhaps he was being a little unkind, he added, "You can pray for the other people later."

Having asked God to look after Klaus, Dani climbed into bed with a peaceful heart and rested his cheek on his hand. But he opened his eyes and said drowsily, " 'Nette?"

"Yes," answered Annette.

"You'll wake me when she comes, won't you?"

"When who comes?"

"Klaus, of course!" And with that, Dani fell asleep.

Annette wandered round the room restlessly, and then, because her cheeks felt hot and because she had been indoors all day, she opened the door and went out onto the balcony.

It had stopped snowing. A west wind was blowing up the valley, piling the snow in drifts against the walls of the chalet. It was not a bitterly cold wind. It felt pleasant on her hot cheeks, and she decided to go for a walk up to the streambed. She might meet Klaus.

She slipped on her cloak and set off. It was a full moon and very light. As Annette reached the top of the field, she turned and looked back over the snow and could see her footprints just like the footprints of the man in her dreams—only his had stretched a long way. He seemed to have traveled right across the world to reach that dark little house—and all for nothing.

17

An Open Door

Annette wandered quite a long way, and at last she reached the little bridge that crossed the stream. The railings were hung with icicles and the stream was almost silent. It was very still up there. The wind had stopped and it had begun to freeze. The little bridge was extremely slippery and Annette never noticed the sheet of ice below the soft snow. Suddenly her foot slipped and she stumbled forward with a little cry of pain.

For a moment the pain in her ankle made her feel faint and sick, and she lay for a minute or two in the snow without moving. Then she tried to get up, but sank down again with another cry, for she had sprained her ankle badly and could not stand on it at all.

For a few minutes she felt terribly frightened. She was alone on the mountainside, and no one was likely to come down that lonely path that night. It was getting colder and colder. Unless she could reach shelter she would certainly freeze to death.

Then she remembered that there was a chalet a little farther up the mountain around the bend in the path, just inside the forest. A young woodsman and his wife lived there. If she could drag herself on her hands and knees to their door, they would take her home on their sled. It was not very far. She would start at once.

She began crawling through the snow, painfully dragging her poor swollen foot behind her. It ached dreadfully at every jolt, and before long she began to get terribly tired. Her hands kept sinking into the snow and her eyes filled with tears. Would she ever get there?

She reached the hairpin bend in the path where the forest started, and to her relief she could see the chalet, not very far away, with one little light in the window.

She struggled on slowly until she reached the steps of the little house. She gave a low call, hoping that someone would come out and carry her up them, but no one came. So she struggled up herself and sank down in an exhausted heap on the doorstep.

Then with a sigh of relief she stretched up and knocked on the door.

There was no answer. The little house seemed as silent as the snow. Annette reached up again and knocked as loudly as she could.

But there was still no answer. Nothing stirred in the little house. No friendly footstep came toward her.

Feeling very afraid, she staggered up on one foot and beat her fists upon the door until they were sore, shouting at the top of her voice and rattling the latch. Then, as the horrid truth dawned on her, she sank down on the steps and burst into frightened tears. The door was locked and the house was empty. The little light had only been left on to scare burglars. There was no one there at all.

For a few minutes she felt in a real panic. She was a mountain child and had often heard stories of people being frozen to death in the snow. But then her panic left her and she began to think more clearly.

If they had left the passage light on, they probably meant to come back that night.

But if they had gone down the valley, they might be a long time coming, and then perhaps it would be too late. Already she could feel the cold creeping into the tips of her fingers.

Perhaps if she rested a little she might be able to crawl back. But the next chalet was a long, long way down, and the snow drifts were soft and deep.

Anyhow, she would wait a little longer and then try. It was her only chance.

She looked hopelessly out into the snowy scene in front of her. Once again she thought of her dream, where there had been footprints all the way to the door of the silent house.

As she sat there waiting, she thought of something else. She knew now, for the first time, what it felt like to knock at a closed door and get no answer.

She had knocked for only a few minutes, but the Lord Jesus went on knocking for years and years. She knew He did.

She had stopped knocking because she knew the house was empty. But just supposing Monsieur and Madame Berdoz had been inside all the time. Suppose they had heard her knocking out in the night and had looked at each other and said, "Somebody's knocking, but we won't let them in just now. We'll pretend not to hear. We won't take any notice!"

How angry she would have been with them. How much she would have hated them for being so unkind!

Yet that was exactly how she was treating the Lord Jesus—and He didn't hate her. He still loved her dearly, or He wouldn't go on knocking and still want to come in. Grandmother had said so.

She was thinking so hard about this that for a moment she almost forgot her fear and loneliness. But she suddenly lifted her head and strained her ears, for she thought she heard a sound.

It was a very gentle sound, but one that all mountain children know well—the sound of skis running through soft snow. Then she heard the sound of a boy's voice, singing.

Someone was coming down through the wood on skis. In a few seconds they would come around the bend and shoot right past the front of the chalet. If they were going very fast, they might not see her.

A little figure came into sight, swaying toward the

valley. Annette kneeled upright and shouted at the top of her voice. "Help!" she cried, cupping her hands in front of her mouth. "Stop and help me!"

The skier turned swiftly and brought his skis to a standstill. Then he unstrapped them and ran lightly up the slope toward her.

"What's the matter?" he cried. "Who is it? Are you hurt?"

It was Lucien. He had been up the mountain to visit his old friend, and now he was on his way home. He had been startled by Annette's cry, and when he saw who it was kneeling there in the moonlight, he stood still and stared as though he had seen a ghost.

But Annette was too pleased to see anyone to care about who it was. Just for a moment she forgot everything except that she was found and saved. She stretched out her hands and seized hold of his cloak as though she was afraid he might run away.

"Oh, Lucien," she cried in a rather shaky voice. "I am *so* glad you've come. I've hurt my foot, and I can't walk, and I thought I might freeze to death before Monsieur and Madame Berdoz came home. Can you take me home, Lucien? I'm getting so cold."

Lucien's big mountain cloak was around her in an instant. He squatted down beside her and rubbed her cold hands.

"I can't take you on the skis, Annette," he said gently, "because you're too big to carry. But I can be home in five minutes, and then I'll come straight back with the big sled and a rug. I'll have you at your chalet in less than half an hour."

Lucien's heart was so full of sudden joy that he felt he must run and shout and sing. His dream had come true. He was doing something useful for Annette. She needed him. Now perhaps she would forgive him and forget that terrible quarrel.

"Won't you be cold without your cloak, Lucien?" asked Annette in a small, exhausted voice.

Lucien promptly took off his jacket and wrapped it around her head, and wished he might give her his shirt as well—although it wouldn't have been the slightest use. He could feel the bite of the frost on his body and raced back over the snow. A moment later he had his skis on and sped off. He felt so happy he hardly noticed the cold. He stumbled into his front door and his mother cried out at the sight of his bare arms and blue nose!

Annette, left alone, snuggled up in the warmth of Lucien's rough cloak. He would be back in about twenty-five minutes, and in those twenty-five minutes there was a good deal to make up her mind about.

First, she was safe. Lucien had come out of the wood just at the right moment, and he had heard her cry. So all the time she had thought she was alone, God had been caring for her and had sent Lucien to save her.

Secondly, she had discovered something about closed doors. She was not quite sure yet just what would happen when she opened the door, but one thing she was quite certain about. She could not leave Jesus outside any longer. She leaned her head against the snowy step rail and closed her eyes.

"Lord Jesus," said Annette, "I'm opening the door now. I'm sorry it's been shut such a long time and you had to wait so long. Please come in now. I'm sorry I've hated Lucien. Please make me love him, and if I've got to tell him about that little horse, please make me brave enough. And thank you for sending Lucien to find me. Amen."

And so the Lord Jesus, who had been waiting outside the door of Annette's heart and life for such a long time, came in. He would forgive her and help her to change. There was no one there to see that wonderful thing happening. Even Annette did not really feel any different. But up in heaven that night, Annette's name was written in God's Book of Life, and the angels rejoiced because another child on earth had opened the door and made room for the Lord Jesus.

18

Things Start to Come Right

Well," thought Annette, "I've done it, and now I know what's got to happen."

She found her heart beating very fast, and she looked up at the vast starry sky and the great mountains to steady herself. How big they were, how old and unchanging! They made her and her fears feel very small and unimportant. After all, it would soon be over and forgotten about, but the mountains and the stars would go on and on forever.

A small black figure appeared, running around the curve in the path, dragging a sled behind him. He had found another coat, and was so out of breath with hurrying that he could hardly speak.

"Come on, Annette," he gasped. "I've brought the big sled so there's plenty of room for you to stretch out your leg. We'll be home in a few minutes."

He held out his hand to help her get up, but she drew back. "Just a minute, Lucien," she said in a hurried, rather shaky voice. "I want to tell you something before we go home. Lucien, it wasn't the cat that knocked over your horse that day. It was me. I did it on purpose because I didn't want you to get the prize—because you hurt Dani. I'm sorry, Lucien."

Lucien stood and stared at her, too surprised and, strangely enough, too happy to speak. For instead of feeling angry, he felt tremendously relieved. Annette had done something wrong as well as him, and if he had to forgive Annette, perhaps it would be easier for Annette to forgive him. Of course a little smashed horse was nothing compared with a little boy's smashed leg, but even so, it seemed to bring them somehow nearer together.

But he couldn't put all that into words, so he just gave a gruff little laugh and said shyly, "Oh, it's all right, Annette. You needn't worry. Get on the sled." Then he tucked the coat around her, sat down in front of her, and together they sped down the mountainside and arrived at the Burniers' front door, powdered all over with the snow that flew up from the runners.

Annette climbed the steps on her hands and knees and stood on one leg in the doorway. Then she looked at Lucien, who was turning away slowly with the sled.

She had opened the door of her heart to the love of the Lord Jesus, and that meant opening the door to

Lucien as well, for Jesus' love never shuts anyone out.

"Come up, Lucien," she called. "Come in and see Grandmother. She will be so pleased that you found me."

She opened the front door as wide as it would go, and she and Lucien went in.

Grandmother jumped up with a cry of joy at the sight of Annette. They had been very worried, and Papa had gone up the mountain to search for her. Grandmother was opening her mouth to be cross when she noticed the lame foot, so she shut her mouth, helped Annette onto the sofa, and went to look for cold-water bandages.

As she turned, she noticed Lucien standing shyly in the doorway, wondering what to do, and for a moment they stood looking at each other. She could see in his face how much he wanted to be accepted, so she put both hands on his shoulders and drew him to the warmth and blaze of the open stove.

"You are welcome, my child," she said firmly. "Come and sit down and eat with us."

The door opened again, and Papa entered, shaking the snow from his cloak. He had guessed Annette was safe, for he had seen the sled and the forms of two children whizzing across the fields. When he had heard her story and scolded her a little for going so far alone at night, he too sat down by the open stove, and Grandmother served out hot chocolate and crusty bread thickly spread with golden butter. On top of each hunk she placed a thick slice of cheese full of holes, and everyone sat munching in silence.

A sleepy, contented silence! The warmth of the stove after the night air made them all feel drowsy. Lucien sat blinking at the flames and wished that this moment could last forever when suddenly the silence was broken by a strange scratching noise at the door.

"It's Klaus," shouted Annette, and she sprang forward. But her bad foot held her back, and it was Grandmother and Papa and Lucien who all opened the door at once.

Klaus marched into the room with her tail held proudly high and in her mouth she carried a perfectly new, blind tabby kitten. She took no notice of any of them, but walked straight across to the little bed where Dani lay sleeping and jumped up onto the feather quilt. She dropped her precious bundle as near as possible to Dani's golden head, and then hurried back to the door and meowed.

"She'll be coming back with another," said Papa, letting her out.

"Then we had better leave the door open," said Grandmother. They all sat shivering in an icy draft until Klaus reappeared in a great hurry and dropped a white kitten with tabby smudges in the same place, and streaked off back into the night.

"Let's hope that will be the last," murmured Grandmother, thinking partly of the draft and partly of life in a small chalet with Dani and more than three kittens. But nobody else said anything at all because their eyes were fixed on the door. Dani's Klaus could do exactly what she liked, and no questions asked.

Back she came around the corner of the barn, but this time she walked slowly and grandly. Her work was done. She carried in her mouth a pure white kitten, exactly like herself, gathered all three between her front paws, laid herself across Dani's chest, and started licking and purring for all she was worth.

"Shut the door, Lucien," said Grandmother with a little sigh of relief. "Pierre, you had better find a basket for all those cats. The child will suffocate!"

Papa chuckled. "In the morning, Mother," he replied. "Tonight they can stop where they are. Klaus knows where they're welcome, and Dani won't mind."

Very gently he moved Klaus's right paw from Dani's chin, then he went off to lock up the cowshed.

Lucien got up to go. He went over to Grandmother and held out his hand.

"I must go," he said simply, "but thank you for letting me come in. I hope Annette's foot will soon be better."

Grandmother, looking down into his face, held his hand for a moment in both of hers. "Yes, you must go," she replied, "but you must come again. You will always be welcome."

Annette said nothing about waking Dani because Grandmother might have said no, but after all, a promise was a promise. She waited until Grandmother was washing up the chocolate cups and then she hopped to his side.

"Dani," she whispered, smoothing the damp hair back from his forehead. Dani sighed and flung his arms above his head but he did not wake.

"Dani," said Annette more loudly, and this time she pinched him. He opened his eyes, bright with sleep, and stared at her.

"Look, Dani," said Annette, "she's come . . . and she's brought you a present!"

Dani stared at the jumble of fur in his arms, too half-asleep to be astonished, and not quite sure whether he was dreaming or not.

"She's found three rats," he remarked.

"No, no, Dani," cried Annette. "Those aren't rats. They are three dear little kittens. She had them in the barn and now she's brought them to you. They're yours, Dani—a present from Klaus."

Dani blinked at them. "I knew she'd come," he murmured. "I asked God."

Annette knelt by the bed and gathered the whole bundle of Dani and Klaus and the kittens into her arms.

"I asked the Lord Jesus to come in," she whispered. "And He did. That's two prayers answered in one night!"

But Dani did not hear. He had fallen asleep again, with the tip of Klaus's tail in his mouth.

19

Annette Wins a Battle

Grandmother's cold-water bandages were so successful that when Annette woke next morning the pain and swelling in her ankle were almost gone. It had snowed in the night, too, and the snow drifts were so deep that Papa had to dig a path to reach the cowshed, so it was not a day for going out.

But Annette and Dani and Klaus and three kittens were just too much for Grandmother, and by afternoon she suggested they should all go over to play in the hay barn.

Dani carried the kittens across in a basket, and Annette lay comfortably on her tummy in the hay with Grandmother's big Bible propped up in front of her.

She wanted to find the verse about Jesus knocking

at the door, and she found it quite quickly, as the pastor had said it came in the last book of the Bible. It was Revelation, chapter 3 and verse 20:

"See, I stand knocking at the door. If anyone hears my voice, and opens the door, I will come in and eat with them, and they with me."

Annette learned it so she could say it without looking, and wondered what the last bit meant about eating together. She must remember to ask Grandmother when she next got a proper chance. Then she lay and watched Dani with his kittens.

She had opened the door to the Lord Jesus and He had come in and was living in her heart, and it had turned out just as Grandmother had said. The hard, angry thoughts had gone away like shadows before the light, and it had suddenly not seemed difficult to forgive Lucien. In fact, the Lord Jesus had shown her how selfish and unloving and untruthful she had been, and what she was really worrying about now was whether Lucien would forgive her.

She had told him about the horse, and he had not seemed cross, but after all, he had lost his prize, and Annette knew now that there was still something more she could do about it, if she really wanted to.

There were the Noah's ark animals. If she took them to the schoolmaster and told him all about it he would see how beautifully Lucien could make things. He would probably give Lucien another prize even now, if he really knew what had happened.

She was so afraid of what the master would think

and what the other children would say that she decided not to do any more about it. But as soon as she decided that, she found she did not want to think about her new book anymore. It had stopped making her happy.

Darkness came early, and the children went in to their evening meal. There was a lot of fuss at bedtime because Dani wanted the kittens to sleep in his bed, and Grandmother wanted them in the barn. In the end they both gave way a little and the kittens ended up sleeping under the bed. Grandmother felt quite tired and sank into her chair with a sigh. As Annette drew up her stool beside her, there was a knock at the door.

Annette got up to open it and Lucien was standing in the doorway, twisting his hands together shyly. Annette felt shy, too, and they both stood there rather awkwardly waiting for each other to say something.

Grandmother looked up, surprised at the silence.

"Come in, Lucien," she called. "We are glad to see you."

They sat down obediently and Lucien said he had come over to see how Annette's foot was. Annette said, "Much better, thank you," while staring at the floor. Grandmother looked at them both very hard over the top of her glasses.

"Annette and Lucien," said Grandmother suddenly, "you must stop this quarrel and behave like sensible children. Lucien, you did a terrible thing, but you did not really mean to do it, and you have suffered for it. It's no good thinking about the past.

Now you must be brave and start again. Annette, you must learn to forgive and be kind, and stop thinking that you are better than other people."

"I don't," said Annette, rather surprisingly. "I have forgiven him—out on the mountain last night. It wasn't very difficult to forgive, because I did something nasty to him as well, and when I told him about it, he said he'd forgive me too, didn't you, Lucien? So we're as bad as each other."

"Yes," replied Lucien simply. "But it wasn't such an awful thing as I did. I can make another horse, but I can't make Dani new legs. And anyhow, everyone says you're good, and likes you, but nobody likes me."

"Perhaps," replied Annette, "it's because they all know what you did, and nobody knows what I did. This afternoon I was thinking I ought to tell the schoolmaster, but somehow I don't think I should ever dare."

They were talking to each other, and Grandmother sat listening, but because it was Grandmother, they did not really mind. Now she spoke.

"Annette," she said suddenly, "how did you come to feel that you could forgive Lucien? Two nights ago you told me you never could."

"Well, Grandmother, I opened the door, like you said, and then it all happened just like you said. When I asked Jesus to come into my heart, somehow it didn't seem so difficult."

"Yes," said Grandmother, "I knew it would be like that if you would only open the door. When Jesus with His great love comes into our hearts, there just isn't room for unkindness and selfishness. There is something else He can get rid of, too. Fetch me my Bible, Annette."

Grandmother turned the pages slowly until she arrived at 1 John, chapter 4, verses 18 and 19. Annette read them aloud, slowly and clearly:

"There is no fear in love; perfect love drives out all fear. . . . We love because God first loved us."

"That's right," said Grandmother. When Jesus brings His perfect love into our hearts, it drives out unkindness and selfishness, and it can also drive out fear. If He loves us perfectly—and He does—He will never let anything really bad hurt us, so there is nothing to be afraid of."

Annette and Lucien sat thinking for a moment, then they smiled at each other. Annette went to the cupboard and fetched her Christmas bear, broke it in half, and gave half to Lucien as a peace offering. They sat on their stools, Lucien munching happily, but Annette still thoughtful and worried. She knew more clearly than ever now what was right, but still she didn't want to do it.

Lucien didn't stay very long, and when he was gone Annette got up to go to bed.

"Annette," said Grandmother, "remember that when Jesus comes in, you must do what He tells you, and not what you want any longer."

"Yes, Grandmother," said Annette rather sadly. She went upstairs and knelt down by her bed to pray.

"Lord Jesus," she said, "I do want to do what You say. If I've really got to tell, please make me brave and stop me being afraid."

Annette got into bed with a lighter heart and soon fell asleep. In the morning she woke early, and as she lay sleepily in the darkness she saw a light creeping through a hole in the shutter. Jumping out of bed, she flung back the shutters and the light streamed in. It filled the little room that had been so dark with the sweet, cold freshness of early morning.

"It's like Grandmother said," thought Annette. "Hating Lucien is like shadows, and being afraid of owning up is like shadows. But letting Jesus in is like opening the shutters."

Then, limping a little, she dressed and went to the kitchen, where Grandmother was stirring the coffee.

"Grandmother," she said firmly, "I want to go and see the schoolmaster this morning."

"What's this all about?" said Papa, who was knocking the snow off his boots in the doorway. "If Annette wants to see the schoolmaster she can come down with me. I'm taking the cheeses down to the train in the mule cart. I'll drop Annette at his house and pick her up on the way back from the station."

Annette's face brightened. If she had had to wait, she might have started feeling terribly afraid again.

Sitting beside Papa in the mule cart, with the cheeses bumping about behind her, and the Noah's ark animals wrapped carefully in a hanky, she didn't feel quite so happy. She couldn't imagine what she would say to the schoolmaster! What if he was very, very angry with her? He might easily be.

"What do you want to see the schoolmaster for?" asked Papa suddenly. "Are you tired of having no lessons to do?"

Annette leaned her head against his coat. "No," she replied shyly. "It's just something I want to tell him. It's a secret, Papa."

She slipped her hand into his as he held the reins. As he was a good, wise man, he just smiled and asked no more questions. He was a very busy man, working hard from early morning till late at night to make his little farm pay enough to keep his children. He did not often have time to talk to them seriously. He left that to Grandmother. But he usually knew what they were thinking by watching their faces and listening to their chatter. In the quiet of the cattle sheds and the forests as he worked for them, he thought about them and prayed for them. He knew that his little daughter had been miserable, and that something had happened and that she felt happy and peaceful, and he was glad.

They jogged on in silence until the white house came in sight. "Down you get," said Papa, "and I'll be back for you in about half an hour."

The mule trotted on, and Annette, with her heart beating very fast, walked up the path, and stood for a long time without daring to knock. She might have stood there until it was time to go home again if the schoolmaster had not seen her out of the window and come and opened the door without her knocking.

"Come in, come in," he said kindly, taking her into the little room where they had so often sat and done lessons together. He loved his students, and in holiday time he missed them and liked them to call on him. Annette went straight to the table and undid her handkerchief and arranged the little Noah's ark animals in a row.

"Lucien made them," she announced firmly. "Aren't they good?"

The master picked them up and examined them with interest. "They are beautifully done," he replied. "They are really exceptional for a boy of his age. He will soon be able to earn his living. I had no idea he could carve like that. Why didn't he enter the handwork competition?"

"He did," answered Annette, still very firmly. "That's what I came to tell you about. He made a little horse, and I smashed it when he wasn't looking because I was so angry about Dani. But I'm sorry now, and I wondered if he couldn't have a prize after all—now that you know all about it."

The schoolmaster looked at her thoughtfully. Her cheeks were scarlet and her eyes fixed on the ground.

"But I haven't another prize," said the school-master at last. "There were only two. One was given to Pierre and one to you."

"Then Lucien ought to have the one that was given to Pierre. It was for the best boy, and Lucien's carving was much better than Pierre's."

"Oh, no," replied the schoolmaster, "we couldn't do that. After all, Pierre won quite fairly. We couldn't take his prize away. If you really want him to have a prize, you will have to give him yours. It was your fault that he lost, wasn't it?"

"Yes," said Annette. And she sat in silence for

three full minutes, thinking. Her prize was a beautiful book full of pictures of all the mountains in Switzerland. It lay in her drawer, wrapped in tissue paper, and was the most precious thing she had.

Of course she could easily say no, and she knew the master would never force her to give it. But Grandmother had talked about perfect love. The Lord Jesus with his perfect love was living in her heart now, and He wouldn't want her to keep anything back.

"All right," said Annette at last.

"Good," replied the schoolmaster, and there was a look of triumph in his eyes because in those three minutes he knew that Annette had won a very big battle. "You shall bring it to me when school begins, and I will present it to him in class, and the children shall see his carvings."

"Very well," said Annette. She looked up shyly into his face to see if he thought her very, very wicked. But he only smiled down at her, and she went away knowing quite well that the old man loved her just as much as he did before.

Back up the hill the empty mule cart bumped and jolted over the snow. Home again, Annette climbed the steps and stood on the veranda, and Dani came and stood beside her with his arms full of kittens. Behind her, Grandmother was cooking the dinner, and in front of her the sun had reached the valley.

"This morning the valley was full of shadows," thought Annette to herself, "and now it's full of sunshine." She knew it was like the Lord Jesus coming into her heart and filling her with love and light and courage.

20

Lucien Has an Idea

Lucien climbed the hill with a light step, and Annette walked by his side. They had never walked home from school together before, but now it was different.

It had been a very happy morning for Lucien. The schoolmaster, without explaining why, had suddenly said that he had seen such a good piece of wood carving over the holidays that he had decided to award another prize. To everyone's astonishment Lucien had been called out to receive it. Annette had expected the schoolmaster to tell the whole story, so she almost fainted with relief when he said nothing about it. Then all the children gathered around to admire the little wooden animals, and freckle-faced Pierre had admired them louder than anyone else, remarking cheerfully that it was lucky for him they were turned in so late or he would never have won the prize. Everyone agreed.

They all wanted to see Lucien's book, and the girls cried out, "Why, it's just the same as Annette's book" – and Annette waited uncomfortably for him to say, "It is Annette's book."

But Lucien only replied, "Is it really?" And when no one was looking, he winked at Annette.

When they were well out of sight of the other children, he held it out to her.

"It was nice getting a prize after all," he said, "but I don't want to keep it. Truly I don't, Annette. It's your book, and I should hate to take it away from you."

Annette shook her head. "No, you've got to keep it," she said. "It's your book now."

"Well," said Lucien, "it really belongs to both of us, so I think we'd better share it. Suppose I have it this month and you have it next month, then me the month after that?"

Annette brightened up. She really wanted her book very badly.

"All right," she replied. "On the first day of every month we'll change."

"Let's sit down on this woodpile and look at it together," said Lucien. They brushed the snow away from the logs and sat down and turned the pages, for Lucien had never seen it before. He was keen on mountains and often studied guidebooks, and now he pointed out to Annette the different ways of climbing them.

They sat there for a long time with the hot midday sun beating down on them and the powder-blue sky behind the white peaks. It was such fun looking at the pictures that they forgot about being late for dinner, until a little voice quite close to them said, "Annette, Granny said I should come and meet you. Dinner's been ready a long time, and I've finished mine."

It was Dani, leaning heavily on his crutches, looking flushed and tired. Annette jumped guiltily off the woodpile.

"Dani," she cried, "you mustn't come so far down the mountain. You'll never get back. We must go home at once."

They started slowly up the road, but Dani was very tired.

He had never been so far alone on his crutches before, but he had kept thinking he would see his sister around the very next corner and had hobbled on. In the end Lucien picked him up and carried him, and Annette carried the crutches.

Lucien carried him right to the door of the chalet, but nobody spoke. A sort of shadow seemed to have come between Lucien and Annette because both were thinking that however much they made up their quarrel Dani was still lame and nothing would give him back his legs.

"My leg aches so," said Dani as Annette carried him up the steps. "Put me on my bed, 'Nette."

So Annette laid him on his bed and gave him all his cats to play with, and she sat down and ate her bowl of cold potato soup. Papa had gone back to his work, and Grandmother, after scolding her for being so late, went to the kitchen where Annette soon joined her. Grandmother was standing at the table skimming rich cream from bowls of milk, and Annette started to help her.

"What is the matter, Annette?" asked Grandmother suddenly. "You look unhappy."

Annette didn't answer for a long time. Then she said, "Grandmother, you said that if I asked Jesus to come into my heart He would make me fond of Lucien, and last week it was all right. But now when I see Dani with his leg hurting so, and remember he used to be so strong, all the bad thoughts come back again."

"Yes," said Grandmother, "I expect they do. Every day of your life, ugly, angry, selfish thoughts will knock at the door and try to get in again. Don't try and push them back yourself. Ask Jesus to help you by filling you with His love. Read about the love of the Lord Jesus every day in your Bible. If you keep your heart full of it, there just won't be room for those bad thoughts to stay."

"Where in the Bible especially?" asked Annette.

"All through the Bible," answered Grandmother. "Read carefully to yourself all the story of the life of Jesus, and think about the way He loved all kinds of people, and remember that it's that same love that came into your heart when you asked Him to come in."

"Yes," answered Annette, and to herself she thought, "I'll start today, and every morning when I wake up, I'll read a story about how Jesus loved someone."

Lucien had gone home to his chalet, also thinking. The sight of Dani so tired made him sad. It was all very well for Annette—she had made up for the wrong things she had done and had put it right. But he could *never* make Dani's legs right.

"Why had Annette forgiven him and been so different?" he wondered for the hundredth time. At first he had thought it was just because he had found her in the snow, but now he knew it was more than that. She had talked about opening a door to Jesus, and Grandmother had said something about the love of Jesus turning out selfishness and unkindness. The old man up the mountain had talked about mercy and forgiveness, too.

Anyhow, opening the door had made a very great difference to Annette. She used to be so proud and unforgiving. Now she was quite humble and kind. It made Lucien think that Jesus was not just someone who lived a long time ago in Bible stories, but someone who really could do things now.

He had been walking slowly, but he had nearly reached the chalet. Twenty minutes before, when he and Annette had sat down on the woodpile, the sky had been blue and still. But now large clouds were massing up behind the mountains, and a cold wind had begun to blow.

"It's blowing up for snow," said Lucien to himself. "There'll be a blizzard tonight."

The cows were stamping restlessly in their stalls at the sound of the wind that had sprung up. Lucien went indoors quickly and joined his mother, who was already eating dinner.

"Come along," said his mother. "You're late. I'm glad you've no afternoon school because it's clouding over and I think we are in for a blizzard. What's that book you've got there?"

"It's a prize," replied Lucien. "The schoolmaster gave it me for carving. He saw something I did over the holidays."

"Well, that was nice of him," said his mother. "Did he know about the other one being smashed?"

"Yes," answered Lucien, and changed the subject. He did not want to answer awkward questions. He was going to keep Annette's secret for her.

His thoughts kept going back to her as he sat in the front room whittling away on some wood held over a newspaper. His mother was ironing in the kitchen so he was alone.

"I asked Jesus to come in." That was what Annette had said. And then Grandmother had read some verses out of the Bible. Perhaps he could find them. He would like to read them again.

He went to the shelf and lifted down the dusty old family Bible. His mother did not often read it, and he only knew what he had learned about it at school. He thought Grandmother's verses had been somewhere near the end. He looked through and found the gospels with the stories he had heard in school about Jesus the healer—how He had made blind men see, and lepers clean, and dead men live; yes, and there was even a story about how He had made someone walk!

Well, if Jesus was really alive today and had

changed Annette's heart, surely He could make Dani walk, too.

Lucien had never really said his prayers since he was a tiny boy and had sometimes said them to his mother. But now he slipped over to the cowshed and ran up into the loft and knelt down on the same spot where all those months before he had hidden and wept so bitterly.

He did not understand yet what it meant to open the door to Jesus, but he believed now that God was near and would listen when he prayed. Now he prayed with all his heart that God would heal Dani and make him walk properly again, as He healed people in the Bible.

He stayed there quite a long time and then slithered down and milked the cows. When he opened the door to cross with the buckets, he was nearly thrown back by the snow driven almost horizontally by the wind. His mother was at the window looking out rather worriedly into the dusk.

"There's a real blizzard on," she said. "You'd better take the storm lantern and go to meet your sister. It's got dark early."

But at that moment the door was flung open and Marie, with snow frozen on her hair and clinging to her coat, stood breathless and laughing in the doorway.

"It was a real fight with the wind getting up that slope," she panted as she shook out her wet clothes and changed her boots. "I'm nearly worn out! Lucien, why didn't you come and meet me with the lantern? Mother, I hope supper's ready, because I'm starving."

They sat down at the table, Marie still chattering gaily, with her cheeks as red as apples.

"What a day I've had," she exclaimed. "People have been coming and going all day at the hotel—not that they'll get much winter sport this weather, poor things! I've been run off my feet, but I got a good tip this evening. Look, Mother."

She pulled out a coin and handed it to her mother. Madame Morel took it with pleased surprise. She, like her neighbors, had difficulty in making the little farm pay, and Marie was a good girl about bringing home her wages.

"Who gave you all that?" she inquired.

"Oh, such a nice man," cried Marie, "and I believe he's very famous, too. The owner's wife was telling me about him at dinner. He's a very clever doctor and he can cure almost anyone with broken bones. He's got a hospital down by the lake, and people go there from all over Switzerland and he cures them."

Lucien nearly choked in his excitement. He leaned across the table. "Marie," he burst out. "could he cure little Dani Burnier?"

Marie stared at him in astonishment. She did not know that Lucien still worried about Dani Burnier.

"I don't know," she answered quite kindly. "They'd have to take him down to the lake if they wanted Monsieur Givet to see him. But they'd never have the money. Those clever men charge huge fees, Lucien, as much as all the Burnier cows put together, I should think."

Down to the lake? To Lucien, who had never left the valley, it seemed like the other end of the world.

He tried again. "But, Marie, couldn't they take him to the hotel in the morning?"

"He's leaving on the early train. All his luggage was brought down tonight."

"Couldn't they take him tonight?"

Marie felt quite sorry for him, but said, "Of course they couldn't, Lucien. Fancy taking a little child out in this blizzard! Anyhow, the last train went hours ago, and the road over the Pass would be blocked on a night like this. It's quite impossible. Besides, I tell you, they haven't the money. Stop worrying yourself about Dani Burnier, Lucien. You didn't mean to harm him, really, and he's quite happy hopping about on that crutch and getting thoroughly spoiled by that grandmother of his!"

Lucien said no more, and his sister went on to talk about the other visitors, but Lucien didn't hear a word. He had quite made up his mind what he was going to do, but there were three mighty difficulties in his way.

The doctor's fees were very high, and Lucien had no money.

His thoughts flew to the old man up the mountain. He had plenty of money if he could be persuaded to give it.

The Pass was probably blocked.

Well, he could try. If he failed, he would know at least that he had done his best.

Would the doctor come? Would he leave the train that would carry him to his important hospital by the lake, and take a local train with a boy he didn't know, and climb the mountain in a blizzard to see a peasant child?

It was all most unlikely, but there was just a chance that he would. Marie had called him a nice man.

"I've finished my supper, Mother," said Lucien. "I'm going upstairs."

21

An Unforgettable Night

Once in his room Lucien moved with great speed. There wasn't a minute to be lost.

He put on his cloak, his woolly hat that came down over his ears, and his strongest boots. Then he wrote a note to his mother telling her he would not be back till morning.

He tiptoed down the stairs into the kitchen and filled his pockets with bread and cheese and a box of matches. Then he silently lifted the latch of the back door and crept to the barn. The storm lantern hung on the wall, and Lucien lit it. The steady light comforted him. He wondered whether to take his skis, but decided it was too dark. He opened the far door of the barn and stepped out into the windy snow meadows, and the blizzard nearly knocked him over.

He was safely away. His great adventure had begun.

If the wind was like this in the field, he wondered what it would be like on the Pass. Surely he would be blown over and buried in the drifts! Well, he would see when he got there. In the meantime he must think hard about reaching the old man.

It was a relief to reach the wood. Here at least he was sheltered and the snow on the path was not so deep, even though the trees made spooky noises. He could move more quickly without falling over.

Up he went through the tossing trees until he could see the orange glow of light in the old man's window. He struggled to the door and knocked.

"Who's there?" said the old man very cautiously from within.

"Me, Lucien."

The door was flung open at once, and the old man helped him inside.

"Lucien, my boy," he cried, peering at him in astonishment, "whatever brings you here in this weather, and at this time of night? What has happened?"

Lucien sank down on the bench for a moment to get his breath back. He did not like asking the old man for his money, but he really needed it badly.

"You once said," began Lucien, looking up into the old man's face, "that you had a lot of money to give to someone if they really needed it. I've found someone who really needs it. If you will give me your money, I think that little Dani Burnier's leg might be made better."

"How could that be?" asked the old man, looking

very closely at the boy.

"There's a doctor at the hotel where my sister works," explained Lucien, "who can cure lame people and heal broken bones. I'm going now to ask him to come and see Dani. But my sister said he would want a lot of money."

"You're going now?" repeated the old man. "In this weather? You must be mad, boy! You could never cross the Pass in this weather."

"I think I could," replied Lucien, "on my skis. The blizzard started only a few hours ago, and the fresh snow won't be deep yet, if I hurry. But it's no good going unless I have the money!"

The old man did not answer for a minute. He seemed to be thinking very hard.

"I would give it if I was sure of the man," he said doubtfully. "But I don't want to waste or lose it. How do I know that he is an honest man? What is his name, Lucien?"

"His name is Monsieur Givet. My sister says he's a famous man."

"Monsieur Givet."

The old man repeated the words softly in a strange voice, as though he thought he must have made a mistake about them. He seemed to have turned rather pale. But without another word he turned away, took a key from one of his own carved boxes, and opened a little cupboard in the wall behind his bed. He took out an old sock stuffed with bills.

"Take it all," he said, "and give it to Monsieur Givet. Tell him it is all his if he will cure the child. Tell him . . . Tell him, Lucien, that it is the payment of a debt."

His voice shook a little, and Lucien glanced at him in surprise, but he was too glad to wonder much. He had never seen so much money before in his life. He put the whole bundle inside his shirt, buttoned his coat and cloak over it, and made for the door.

"Thank you very much," he said hastily at the door. "I'll come and tell you what happens."

The old man came to the door to watch him go and held his lantern high to light the path. Lucien had gone only a few steps when the old man called to him loudly above the wind. "Lucien!"

Lucien ran back. "Yes, Monsieur?"

"You won't forget the message, will you?"

"No," replied Lucien carefully. "I'm to say it's the payment of a debt. I won't forget. Good-bye, Monsieur."

He was making off again into the night when the old man called again. "Lucien."

The boy ran back, feeling impatient now. He wanted to get going. "Yes, Monsieur?"

"You won't tell him anything about me, will you? Don't tell him my name, will you, Lucien?"

"I don't know your name," Lucien reminded him.

"And don't tell him where I live!"

"No, Monsieur," Lucien answered him, too impatient to wonder why. "I'll just say it's the payment of a debt. Good-bye, Monsieur."

He sped off as fast as he could through the deep, soft snow, afraid that the old man might call him again. At the edge of the wood he turned and waved his lantern. Through the whirling snow he could still see the dim figure of the old man, black against the light of his open door.

He must be very quick. The snow was still falling. Very soon the Pass would be impossible to cross, if it was not so already.

He thought it probably would be impossible to cross on foot, so he decided to stop in at the wood-shed on his way down and get his skis.

He had just lifted his skis down when the far door of the cowshed was flung open and his mother and Marie came in, waving a lantern. Lucien propped his skis against the wall and fell flat on his face on the dirty floor behind the largest cow.

"He's not here," said his mother in a sharp, worried voice, flashing her lantern around the shed. "I believe you're right, Marie. He's got some mad idea about going to that doctor. He'll be stumbling along that mountain road by now, and the stupid boy hasn't even taken his skis. I wonder if we could persuade Monsieur Burnier to go after him and fetch him back. He can't have got far on foot."

"I think we'd better," agreed Marie. Her voice sounded worried, too. "Monsieur Burnier will easily catch up with him on skis and stop him before he gets anywhere really dangerous. Let's go now and ask him."

They went off hastily, and Lucien, pressed against the cow's body, jumped to his feet. There wasn't a moment to lose.

It would take them two or three minutes to get on their coats and boots. In this weather it would take them fifteen minutes to reach the Burnier chalet.

Another ten minutes while they told their story and Monsieur Burnier collected his lantern and boots and skis. Lucien worked out he had roughly half an hour's start. It should be enough, but then he was only a light child, and Monsieur Burnier was a heavy, skillful man who could ski much faster than Lucien.

Very, very carefully he crept out from the cowshed, relit the lantern, and fastened on his skis. Carefully he started off, keeping his head down because the blizzard was blinding.

Down over the meadows, he once again reached the friendly shelter of the forest path where he could look in front of him. Out across the low fields he sped, and here the wind was less furious and he could look straight ahead.

He made his way through the deserted village, looking around worriedly in case anyone should see him and want to know what he was doing. But everyone was indoors on such a night. He crossed the silent market square with its frozen fountain, past the dairy, over the bridge, and then he paused for breath. He glanced back fearfully in case Monsieur Burnier should be following, but there was no one in sight.

Now he had reached the lowest part of the valley and must start the climb up over the Pass that ran between two mountains. He suddenly felt terribly lonely, and for a moment he almost wished Monsieur Burnier would catch up. But he pushed the thought away and began his climb.

The snow on the valley road was not too bad.

Lucien put his skis over his shoulder and found he could walk without much difficulty. The blizzard seemed to be stopping.

Once again he went into the woods and climbed, weary and afraid. These were dark, strange woods that he did not know and he was not even sure if he was on the right path. If he wasn't, it might lead to a precipice. He could hear the howling wind and a rushing stream above him, and his skis seemed heavier and heavier.

He climbed through the woods for three hours, his mind full of fears and horrors of all the dangers that were to be found on the mountains: avalanches, treacherous snow drifts, breaking tree boughs. He thought of the St. Bernard dogs trained to rescue lost travelers.

Of course, he could go back.

He stopped for a moment wondering why that thought had not occurred to him before. How simple it would be to buckle on his skis and zigzag down the forest path and go home.

"I did my best," he would tell them, "but I couldn't get through." The Burniers would no doubt think he was very brave to have even tried.

The wind was roaring horribly now, and the great trees seemed to be crying aloud and tossing their arms. He was nearly at the top of the forest, out on the wild wastes of the Pass where the wind might pick him up and whirl him over the rocks like a snowflake. He found his teeth were chattering, and he was crying.

"I'm so frightened," he sobbed to himself. "I can't

go on. I know I'll be killed on the Pass. I wish Monsieur Burnier would come."

As he stooped to buckle on his skis, he suddenly remembered that warm, sheltered moment when he and Annette and Grandmother sat around the stove together and Grandmother had talked about being afraid.

"Perfect love drives out fear. If we really believe Jesus loves us perfectly there is nothing left to be afraid of. If he loves us perfectly He will never let anything really harm us."

Lucien realized he was not alone after all. Grandmother had said that Jesus loved him perfectly, and if He loved perfectly He would not leave a child alone in darkness and danger. It was just as though someone stronger than the night, the wind, the terror, and the darkness had suddenly come to him and taken his hand and pointed up the mountain.

Lucien decided to go on.

"Perfect love drives out fear," he murmured to himself over and over again. It was true, too. He had stopped feeling so terribly frightened because he had stopped feeling alone.

He had reached the top of the forest and come out into the open, and now he could think of nothing at all except how to go on.

He struggled on, foot by foot, bent nearly double because the pain of the cold wind on his face was more than he could bear. At times the snow was over his knees, but he kept going. One icy blast knocked him onto his back and he feared he wouldn't be able to get up again, but a little strength seemed to return and he struggled to his feet again. At last he found that the ground in front of him sloped gently downward and he knew he had crossed the Pass.

Soon he reached forest again and the wind dropped. He felt numb with cold. Thankfully he realized he had not missed his way. God had certainly been guiding him.

He zigzagged carefully through the trees on the forest track, feeling glad to be sheltered from the wind that had beaten the sense and feeling out of him.

Down – down – down. The forest was almost quiet now, for he was traveling toward a deep valley. When at last he glided out into the open, the fields lay still and silver in the moonlight, and the dark town was below him. In half an hour's time he would be there, knocking on the door of the great hotel, and then . . .

"If Jesus really loves me perfectly," thought Lucien, "He can't have let me come all this way for nothing." Too tired to think anymore, he set out across the meadows toward the town.

22

Lucien Finds Monsieur Givet

Monsieur Givet woke very early, and the first thing he thought of was that the storm had stopped and the valley was still. The second thing he remembered was that he was going home today.

He was glad he was going home. He had been ill and had come up to the mountains for a week's rest and mountain air. Now he felt strong again and ready for work, and today he would travel on the early train and reach his lakeside home before mid-day—and what a welcome there would be!

What a noise the children would make. He smiled as he thought of them. He had two boys and two girls, who wore their poor mother out. He wished he could find someone who would help her with them.

He got out of bed and whistled while he shaved.

Just as he was finishing there was a knock on the door.

"Come in," called Monsieur Givet, surprised, for it was much too soon for the early breakfast he had ordered. It was only about half past five.

The door opened and the night porter came in. He looked as though he had some rather mysterious news.

"Excuse me, sir," he began, tilting his head to one side, "but you weren't by any chance expecting a visitor?"

"A visitor?" echoed Monsieur Givet, even more surprised, "at this hour and in this weather? I certainly am not."

"Well, sir," said the porter, "it's like this. Just a quarter of an hour ago I heard a little tap on the door, and when I opened it, there on the steps stood a boy on skis, about twelve years old, sir, white as a sheet and looking more like a ghost than a boy. 'I want Monsieur Givet,' he said, without even stopping to say good morning. Then he sat down on the step and leaned his head against the doorway.

" 'Well,' I said to him, 'you can't come calling on people at this hour of the morning, laddie. He's asleep in his bed.'

" 'I'll wait, then,' he said, and his head sank down onto his knees.

"Well, I don't like to see a child like that, so I took off his skis and dragged him in and sat him on a chair. 'Where have you come from?' I asked him.

" 'From Pré d'Oré,' he said.

" 'How's that?' I asked. 'The early train isn't in yet.'

" 'I came over the Pass,' he said. And Monsieur, the more I look at that boy the more I feel like believing him. He's sitting down in the hall now, and when I passed your door, sir, and saw the light on, I thought I'd come in and ask if you'd like to see him."

"I'll come and see him, certainly," answered Monsieur Givet, "but I really can't believe that story about him coming over the Pass. I don't believe the mountain guides themselves could have crossed last night. It must have been terrible up there."

The porter shrugged his shoulders and led the way downstairs When they reached the hall they both ran forward with a cry of dismay.

The boy had slithered off the chair and lay in a dead faint on the floor. His face looked strangely white.

Monsieur Givet picked the unconscious child up in his arms. "I'll take this boy to my room," he said to the alarmed porter. "You bring me some hot water bottles and some brandy and coffee, and be as quick as you can."

Upstairs in his room he laid the boy on his bed, removed his sodden boots and socks, and rubbed his numb feet. Then he took off his snowy clothes and wrapped him in blankets. By this time the night porter had arrived, puffing very hard, with the bottles and the brandy and the steaming coffee.

Monsieur Givet arranged the bottles and held a teaspoonful of brandy to Lucien's white lips. He did not open his eyes, but gave a tired sigh and swallowed the brandy.

"That's right, laddie," said Monsieur Givet.

"You'll soon be around."

When Lucien opened his eyes a few minutes later, he looked straight up into a kind brown face, and couldn't think where he was. He felt so warm and comfortable and sleepy, he thought he would never want to move again as long as he lived. But he would like to know who the man with the kind brown face was, who looked at him so closely.

"Who are you?" he murmured.

Monsieur Givet didn't answer at once. He raised Lucien's head and gave him hot coffee. Lucien swallowed very slowly because it seemed too much of an effort to swallow just at the moment. When he had finished, he said again, "Who are you, and where am I?"

"I'm Monsieur Givet," replied the doctor. "I don't know you, but I understand that you wanted me."

Lucien stared at him rather stupidly. He had been so tired that he had almost forgotten what he had come for. But with the warmth and the food things were beginning to get clear again, and at last he spoke.

"Are you a great, clever, famous doctor?"

"No, I'm just a doctor."

"But can you make lame children walk?"

"It depends on why they are lame. Sometimes I can."

"He's lame because he fell over a precipice. He walks with a crutch and a big boot."

"Who does?" asked the bewildered Monsieur Givet.

"Little Dani Burnier. He's six. He lives in the

chalet next to mine. I came to ask if you could make him well. I've got enough money to pay you."

"How did you hear of me?"

"My sister told me about you last night. My sister is a maid here."

"How did you get here in that storm?"

"I came over the Pass on my skis."

"You couldn't have done that, boy, not in that blizzard."

"But I did. There's no other way to come."

It was quite true. Monsieur Givet sat looking at the boy as though he were something from another planet. As the doctor stared, Lucien's hand crept under the shirt he was still wearing and took out the fat stocking.

"Please, sir," he said, "would this be enough to make him better?"

Monsieur Givet emptied the stocking and gave a cry of astonishment.

"My boy," said Monsieur Givet quite gently but very firmly, "before we go any further you must tell me where you got all this money from. Do you know how much there is?"

"No," said Lucien rather drowsily. "But my sister said you'd want a lot. Is it enough?"

"That depends on whether you want to buy my clinic as well," replied the doctor. "It's far too much. Where did you get it from?"

"An old man I'm friends with gave it to me," murmured Lucien, who felt he could not keep his eyes open another minute, "and there was a message. He said it was the payment of a debt, and you were to take it all."

"Who was this old man?" asked Monsieur Givet. "Just tell me that, and then you shall go to sleep. What is his name?"

"Please, sir, I don't know."

"Where does he live?"

"He made me promise not to tell you." With that, Lucien's eyes closed and his head rolled over to one side. He fell fast asleep.

Monsieur Givet was in rather an awkward situation. His train was due to leave in three-quarters of an hour. But the boy lying on the bed had risked his life to come to him. It might be all for nothing, but he couldn't disappoint such a brave child by refusing to see the little cripple. Yet the lad would probably sleep for hours now.

He left the room softly, went downstairs to the telephone, and rang his wife.

"Are you there, Marthe?" he began. "Darling, I'm so sorry, but I shan't be home till tomorrow. Such a strange thing has happened." And he told her the whole mysterious story.

As he left the office he was nearly knocked over by a red-eyed, pale-faced girl in outdoor clothes. She caught hold of his hand.

"Oh, sir," she cried, "Porter tells me you've got my little brother safe upstairs. Mother and I thought he was dead in the drifts. I must go home quick and tell my mother he's here."

Monsieur Givet sat down beside her on a sofa and tried to get some sort of explanation out of her, but she could talk of little but the terrible night she and her mother had passed through.

Marie could tell Monsieur Givet very little about Dani. She was too upset to work, and now that she knew Lucien was safe she was in a hurry to take him home. She would telephone the post office now, and they would get a child to run up the mountain with the news so that her mother would hear more quickly.

But Monsieur Givet would not hear of Lucien going home just yet. Marie could go home by herself, and when Lucien woke he would bring him on the train. Marie had better get someone to send a mule sleigh to the station, as Lucien would probably be too stiff to walk.

Marie agreed to everything and made off as fast as she could while Monsieur Givet went back to his room. Lucien still lay just as he had left him, with his cheek resting on his hand But there was a faint tinge of color in his face. He looked much better. Monsieur Givet sat down and watched him and wondered again how the boy had got all that money. Who was the old man who had sent such a strange message?

"The payment of a debt!" Monsieur Givet decided to look into the matter very closely.

Lucien woke at midday, and once again could not remember where he was for quite a long time. He was aching all over and didn't want to move. Monsieur Givet heard a little movement and came to see what was happening.

"Well," he asked kindly, "how do you feel?"

"All right, thank you," answered Lucien. Then he

remembered that he'd been to sleep and added worriedly, "Will you have time to see the little boy I told you about, sir?"

"Yes," said Monsieur Givet, sitting down beside him. "We'll go after dinner. I'll ring now for them to send up dinner for two, and while we eat you can tell me all about this little boy and all about this old man whom you say sent the money."

"I can't tell you about the old man, sir," replied Lucien, "because I promised not to. He's a sort of secret, and no one ever goes to see him except me. He said I was just to tell you it was the payment of a debt and nothing else at all, sir. And he's been so kind to me, I couldn't break my promise."

"All right," said Monsieur Givet. "You shan't break your promise. I won't ask you anything more about him. Tell me about this little cripple. When did he hurt himself, and how did it happen?"

Lucien went very red. He didn't answer for a few minutes. He didn't want to tell his new friend what had really happened, but as Monsieur Givet would be sure to find out from the Burniers, it might be better if he heard it first from Lucien. So he replied, "It was my fault, really. It was last spring. I was teasing him. I pretended to drop his kitten over the ravine, then by mistake I really did drop it. Dani tried to rescue it and fell and hurt his leg, and since then he's never walked properly—only with crutches—and I thought perhaps . . ."

His lips trembled and his voice trailed off miserably into a whisper. But he had said enough. For the doctor loved and understood children, and in those few broken sentences he had understood the whole story. He knew that this tired boy lying on the bed had been punished very bitterly.

"Lucien," he said, "we'll see this child together. It may be that God is going to make you the means of curing him. You know, Lucien, you have a great deal to thank God for. I think He must have been looking after you in a very special way last night or you would never have come across the Pass alive."

"Yes, I know," answered Lucien shyly and eagerly. "You see, only yesterday I prayed that God would make Dani better. Then when I heard about you, I thought it was the answer. But when I got to the forest, I felt frightened and nearly went back, but I remembered something I heard at Christmas and thought I'd go on instead."

"What did you remember?" asked Monsieur Givet gently.

"I remembered some verses in the Bible that Dani's grandmother read to us," answered Lucien slowly. "I can't remember it all, but it said that perfect love drives out fear. And Grandmother said Jesus' love was perfect, so I wasn't afraid and I went on. I can't remember much about the journey, but I got here safely."

"Yes," replied Monsieur Givet. "I don't think anything but the perfect love of the Lord Jesus could have sheltered you in that storm or guided you on the right road or kept you from being too afraid to go on. He's been very, very good to you, Lucien. Let's thank Him now, before our dinner comes."

Lucien buried his face in the pillow, and Monsieur

Givet knelt by the bed and prayed. He thanked God for His perfect love that is stronger than storm or blizzard, which had guided Lucien's steps through the darkness and saved him from fear and death. Then he prayed for little Dani, that God would give him, the doctor, skill to heal that lame leg.

Lucien, with his face in the pillow, prayed as well, only not out loud "Lord Jesus," he cried in his heart, "You were near me on the mountain and I wasn't afraid. Don't go away again. I want to open my door like Annette did. Please come in."

23

Dani Meets the Doctor

Monsieur Burnier met the mule train himself, with his own mule sleigh, and drove Monsieur Givet and Lucien up to the chalet. All the villagers came to their front doors to see the famous doctor pass, as everyone had heard the story. They were all talking about Lucien as if he was a great hero for being so brave to cross the Pass as he did.

Monsieur Burnier sat silently in the driver's seat, not knowing what to think about it all. It was rather a responsibility having such a famous man on that sleigh. He only hoped the mule, who was very frisky that day, wouldn't tip the sleigh over the edge on one of the bends, which often happened.

He was worried about the money, too. Of course he would give every penny he had to see Dani cured, but he didn't have many pennies, and what if they weren't enough? Perhaps this very famous man would accept a young bull by way of payment.

Fortunately, they reached the chalet without any adventures or upsets, and Monsieur Burnier helped the doctor get down and then lifted poor Lucien in his strong arms and carried him up the steps and into the front room, where he laid him on the couch. He, too, was pleased to see Lucien, for he had spent a long, weary night searching for him in the drifts.

Grandmother, Annette, and Dani looked rather odd, as though they were about to have their photo taken. They were all dressed in their very best clothes, sitting in a stiff little group on the edge of the best chairs. They looked as though they had been sitting there expecting the very famous man for a long time. When he came in, Annette and Dani looked at Grandmother and stood up politely.

Dani was not at all pleased. He had thought that a very famous man would be dressed in a red robe like the governor who made William Tell shoot the apple off his son's head, in Annette's Swiss history book. This stranger who came in behind Papa didn't look very special at all.

The doctor sat on a chair as far away as possible from the group and smiled at them. He had a nice broad smile, and Dani forgot his disappointment and smiled back.

Monsieur Givet put his hand in his pocket, took out a sweet, and held it out.

"Would you like a sweet, Dani?" he asked.

Dani grinned happily and nodded his head hard.

"Come and fetch it, then," said Monsieur Givet, and Dani hopped delightedly across the room while the doctor watched him very closely. When the child reached him, he lifted him onto his knee and put the sweet in his mouth.

He really liked this family—especially this chuckling, friendly, blue-eyed little boy who sat noisily sucking a sweet on his lap. He noticed, too, that there was no mother, and wondered whether it was the old woman or the little girl who kept the chalet looking so neat and tidy.

"Does your leg hurt?" asked Monsieur Givet.

"No," answered Dani.

"No, *Monsieur*," corrected Grandmother.

"Monsieur," added Dani. "Only sometimes, when I walk without my crutches. My crutches have got bears' heads on them. Would you like to see them?"

"Very much indeed," said Monsieur Givet, and as Dani hopped over to fetch them he again watched him very closely.

"I can do enormous great hops on my crutches," announced Dani proudly. "Would you like to see me?"

"Very much indeed," answered the doctor again.

"Be careful of the chairs, Dani," said Grandmother quickly, for she had forbidden Dani to do enormous great hops in the house. Annette quickly picked up two kittens, as she wasn't sure where Dani would land.

The hop was a huge success, and the doctor clapped his hands. "Well done," he cried. "That was exactly like a kangaroo I once saw at the zoo. Now put down your crutches and walk to me without them."

Dani limped toward him, smiling, but dragging his lame leg rather pitifully. Monsieur Givet smiled back, lifted the little boy very gently onto his knee again, and gave him another sweet.

Grandmother, who had been watching very closely, turned to Annette.

"Annette," she said, "put the kettle on and make a pot of tea and bring out the biscuit tin."

While Annette was getting the tea, Monsieur Givet laid Dani flat on the table and twisted and turned his leg about for a long time. In fact, when he had finished the tea was ready and Grandmother invited him to sit down and drink with them. He seemed to be thinking hard.

"Well," said Grandmother at last, rather sharply, "can you do anything for him?"

Every eye in the room was fixed on him as they waited for his answer—except for Dani, whose eyes were fixed on the biscuits, because they had forgotten to pass him one and Grandmother would be cross if he got up and helped himself. They were special bricelet biscuits—thin, crisp, golden and delicious, and Grandmother made them once a month on a special grill.

Monsieur Givet did not answer at once. He turned to Dani instead.

"Dani," he said, "would you like to be able to run about like other little boys?"

Dani hesitated. He was not quite sure. He was the only boy in the village who had bear crutches, and it made him a very special person. Then he remembered that spring was coming, and unless he could run about he would not be able to chase the baby goats in the meadows as he had done last year. And chasing baby goats was such good fun.

So he said, "Yes, thank you, I would. And please, Grandmother, may I have a bricelet biscuit?"

No one answered. Lucien and Annette were sitting with their cups held in midair and both were rather pale. Everyone was still staring at Monsieur Givet.

"Dani," said the doctor suddenly, "where's that fine cat gone?"

"To the woodshed," said Dani. "Would you like to see her? She's got three kittens."

"Yes, please," answered Monsieur Givet, and Dani limped off to find Klaus, helping himself to two bricelet biscuits as he passed the table, but nobody seemed to notice.

As soon as the door had closed on Dani, Monsieur Givet turned to Papa.

"I think I may be able to help you," he said, leaning forward and speaking very earnestly, "although I can't tell for certain until I've seen an X-ray of it. I think the bone was never set properly and has joined up wrongly, but I could break it again and pull it out straight. It would mean an operation and a long stay in the hospital. Would you be willing to let him come?"

Papa rubbed his hands together miserably and looked helplessly, first at Grandmother and then at Annette. He had no experience with operations and the word sounded horrible. Besides, he had been told that operations were expensive, and he wouldn't be able to pay.

"How much would it cost?" he asked at last, scratching his head.

"It wouldn't cost you anything," replied Monsieur Givet. "Lucien has paid for it himself, in any case. I can't explain now because Dani will be back and we must decide before he comes. Will you let me take him?"

"Yes," replied Grandmother, who hadn't been asked.

"When?" inquired Annette.

"Tomorrow morning," replied Monsieur Givet. "I shall be catching the early train, and can take Dani with me."

"Where am I going on the train?" said a clear voice. Dani had come in quietly through the back door and no one had noticed him. Now he stood at Monsieur Givet's elbow with an armful of kittens, looking pleased. He had only been on a train once in his whole life just for ten minutes, but he had never forgotten it.

No one answered. They were still staring at Monsieur Givet.

"Where, Grandmother?" asked Dani again.

The doctor turned to Dani. "Dani," he said, "you're coming with me down to the lake, and you're going to stay with me for a while, and I hope I'm going to make your leg better. Would you like that?"

Dani looked as if he wasn't too sure about it. "And Annette?" he asked firmly. "And Grandmother and

Papa and Klaus and the kittens? Yes, Monsieur, we shall all like it very much."

"Oh, no, Dani," cried Annette. "We can't all go; you've got to be good and go by yourself. Monsieur Givet will look after you and you'll soon come back." She was nearly crying herself.

The effect of these words was terrible. Dani flung himself, kittens and all, into Annette's arms and burst into tears, making the most deafening noise.

Never had they heard such a row. Annette hugged and kissed him, Grandmother tried to soothe him, and Papa pressed handfuls of bricelet biscuits into his clenched fists, but nothing helped. The family looked at each other helplessly. Monsieur Givet knew he had to think of something very quickly.

He turned to Grandmother. "Does the little girl know anything about looking after children?" he shouted above the din.

"She brought up this one," shouted back Grandmother.

"You had better send her with her little brother then," yelled Monsieur Givet. "She can help my wife."

"Dani," shouted Annette, shaking him to make him listen, "I'm coming, too!"

Dani stopped at once, gave three hiccups, and smiled. Monsieur Givet did not smile back. He picked up the little boy and spoke to him seriously.

"I'm afraid you are very spoiled, Dani," he said. "When you come to my hospital, you will have to do what you are told without any fuss or screaming." He put Dani down. "I am going to take Lucien home if you can lend me a sled," he said. "So I will say good-bye for now. The two children will meet me on the platform at 8:30 tomorrow morning with all that they need for the next two or three months. Annette shall help my wife in the mornings and go to evening classes for her schooling. In the afternoons she can be free to be with her little brother."

Papa shook hands dumbly and wiped his brow. Things were moving so fast that he felt he had been left behind. But he was beginning to understand that for two months, starting tomorrow, he had to live without Annette and Dani in a silent, tidy chalet. He went stumbling over to the cowshed to milk and try to think things out.

Grandmother said good-bye at the door, and held the doctor's hand for some moments. "You are a good man," she said suddenly. "God will reward you."

Monsieur Givet looked at the brave old woman in front of him. He saw her with her two happy, healthy grandchildren behind her and the clean, peaceful home of which she was the guardian angel. He knew she was strengthened by love and courage and realized she was a very special person.

"You, too," he replied, "are a good, unselfish woman and will most certainly find your reward."

Monsieur Givet pulled Lucien to his own chalet on a borrowed sled and carried him to his mother. She pretended to be very angry with him.

"You naughty boy, Lucien," she cried, "going off like that and giving us all such a dreadful fright. How could you do such a thing? You deserve a beating." She took him almost roughly from Monsieur

Givet's arms, helped him up the stairs, and put him to bed herself. Then she came back, sat down at the table, flung her black apron over her face, and began to cry.

"You have a very brave son, Madame," said Monsieur Givet.

"He's a very naughty boy," snapped Madame, and because she was so terribly proud of him and so glad to see him safe, she began to cry worse than before.

She and Marie had been baking a big batch of Lucien's favorite cakes all morning, and the house was full of the good smell. They invited Monsieur Givet to sit and eat with them, but he refused because he still had something important to do and time was getting on.

"I believe," he began rather sharply, "that Lucien knows some old man around here. Can you tell me where he lives?"

"An old man?" repeated Marie. "Oh, yes, that would be the old man up the mountain who teaches Lucien wood carving. They spend hours together, although what Lucien sees in him, goodness knows! Most people say he's crazy."

"Can you tell me the way to his house?" asked Monsieur Givet.

"Why, yes," replied Marie, surprised. "It's straight up through the forest. But I shouldn't go up there if I were you, sir. The path will be bad after all this snow."

"I have business with him," replied Monsieur Givet. "Perhaps you will point out the path to me from the door. On the way down I will come and say good-bye to Lucien."

Monsieur Givet thought how beautiful the forest looked as he toiled up the track that late afternoon. What must it be like, he thought, to be that old man and live alone among all this silence and peace, sharing the secrets of the forest. He began to look forward to meeting him and found his heart was beating faster than usual.

As he left the forest he could see the hut standing halfway up the meadow, with the snow piled high against its walls. The old man had dug a little path as far as the trees—almost as though he was expecting a visitor, thought Monsieur Givet, picking his way along it.

He knocked softly on the door and went in without waiting for a reply. The old man sat hunched up over his stove, whittling wood and smoking his pipe. A goat and a cat sat on each side of him for company, and Monsieur Givet sat on the chair on the other side of the stove.

"Well," said the old man, still not looking up, "did you get there safely, Lucien?"

"It's not Lucien," replied Monsieur Givet softly, and the old man jumped and looked up. They sat staring at each other as though they had each seen a ghost—and yet uncertainly, as though the ghost might possibly be real after all.

"I have come to give you back this money," said Monsieur Givet at last. "I don't want money to help that child. Under the circumstances I will do it free, if it can be done."

"Then the boy broke his promise," growled the old

man. He leaned his chin on his stick and stared and stared and stared.

"He did not break his promise," replied Monsieur Givet. "He told me nothing except that it was given him by an old man and that it was the payment of a debt. But I do not accept large sums of money from peasant boys without making sure that they were come by honestly. I had no difficulty in finding out from other people who you were and where you lived."

There was another long, long silence. "Is that all you came to say?" said the old man at last. His voice sounded suddenly old and weary and hopeless.

Monsieur Givet got up quickly and knelt down beside the bowed figure of the old man.

"Need we pretend any more?" he asked. "Surely we are both quite sure of each other. I've come to take you home, Father, and to tell you how much we've missed you and wanted you."

24

Jesus' Love Makes All the Difference

A few hours later Annette sat in a big wooden rocking chair, smiling at Lucien, who was sitting up in bed. He was still rather pale and tired, but otherwise well and happy.

"Tell me all about it," urged Annette, her eyes big with admiration and astonishment. "Everyone says it was so brave of you. Tell me right from the beginning, Lucien, and what it was like on the top of the mountain."

It was nice to be called brave, and Lucien would have liked to make a good story of it, but somehow it all seemed very far away and difficult to talk about—almost as if it had been a dream.

"Well," he began, "I went up to the old man first and asked him for some money, and then I got my skis on the way down and skied down the valley and climbed through the woods across the river, and then I went down the other side."

"Of course you did," interrupted Annette impatiently, "or you'd never have got there. But tell me about it properly, Lucien. What did you feel like? Did you have any adventures? Were you frightened, and did you nearly die? What was it like on the top?"

Lucien was silent for a few moments. All afternoon he had been wondering whether there would be a chance to tell Annette, but now the chance was here and he didn't know how to begin.

"Yes," he said at last, rather slowly, "I was very frightened a little way before the top. I nearly came back. Annette, do you remember telling me how you used to hate me so much, and how you asked Jesus into your heart and He made you like me instead?"

"Yes," replied Annette eagerly, "of course I remember. Why, Lucien?"

"Because," went on Lucien shyly, "something like that happened to me when I was feeling so frightened. I remembered those verses your grandmother taught us about perfect love driving out fear, and I asked Jesus to take away mine, and I stopped feeling so terribly afraid almost at once."

"Did you really?" asked Annette, deeply interested. "Then I suppose Jesus came into your heart as well as mine, and then your being afraid had to go away just like my hating had to go away. I suppose it's all really the same, Lucien. Whether you're afraid or don't like people, or whether you cheat or don't speak the truth, or you are lazy or cross—whatever's the matter with you, when Jesus comes in, I suppose there just isn't room for it anymore."

"Yes," agreed Lucien thoughtfully, and they sat and talked about it for quite some time.

It was not until Annette was walking home across the snow that she fully realized that this was her last evening at home for a long time, and it suddenly made her feel very sad. She ran home quickly.

Papa was still over in the cattle shed, but Grandmother was sitting sewing a button on Annette's clean pinafore dress. Their clothes, neatly folded and mended, were tied in two bundles on the table all ready for morning. Dani lay fast asleep in the bed in the corner with all his kittens on top of him as a last treat.

"Grandmother," cried Annette, and she ran straight into the old woman's arms and burst into tears.

Grandmother let her cry for a little, then she pulled up the stool and Annette sat down and leaned against Grandmother's knees while the old lady talked. She talked about the home Annette was going to, the work she would have to do, and how good it would be to see Dani made well. She talked so bravely that Annette never knew that deep down in her heart Grandmother was saying to herself, "What shall I do tomorrow night and all the nights after when the stool at my feet is empty and there's no sleeping little boy in the bed in the corner?"

Then, because it was getting late and they must be up early, Annette fetched the big Bible down from the shelf, as she always did at bedtime, and read aloud to Grandmother.

"We'll read first Corinthians chapter thirteen tonight," said Grandmother as Annette rested the great Book on her knees. "It's a chapter I would like you to remember all the time you're away."

Annette read it right through, and when she had finished, Grandmother said, "The verse I want you to really remember is verse four—

"Love is patient and kind; it is not jealous or conceited or proud."

"Now," said Grandmother, looking at Annette over her glasses, "you tell me you have asked Jesus into your heart, and He has come in and brought His love with Him—the kind of love we were reading about. You are going to look after children, and they won't always be good. When they are naughty and you feel cross and impatient with them, ask Jesus to help you.

"You are going to a big house, Annette, and you will see nice things that you will probably never have yourself. Sometimes you may feel jealous and unhappy about it. But remember, if your heart is full of love, there won't be room for jealousy.

"You are going to be a little servant in a busy household. I don't expect you will get much notice taken of you. But remember, the love of Jesus in you never pushes itself forward and never looks for attention. His love can make you go on doing your work quietly and faithfully whether anyone notices you or not. Remember, He is your master and you are working to please Him."

"I'll try to remember, Grandmother," said Annette thoughtfully, then she kissed her and ran across to the cattle shed to spend the last half an hour before bed with Papa.

Early next morning the whole family drove to the station in the mule cart and arrived half an hour too early because they were so afraid of missing the train. They stood on the platform among the milk churns waiting for Monsieur Givet, who soon joined them. Annette carried their luggage in a brown paper parcel, and her hand was clasped tightly in her father's.

Dani, in his cloak and hood, seemed unusually shy and kept edging off behind the milk churns. He seemed nervous and didn't want to be hugged when it came to say good-bye. The train was far down the valley before Annette understood why. Then she noticed strange movements under Dani's cloak, as if he was having hiccups.

"What is that under your cloak, Dani?" she asked, gazing in astonishment at it.

Dani went pink.

"It's only one, 'Nette," he replied nervously.

"One what?" inquired Annette, glancing worriedly up at Monsieur Givet. But the doctor was reading a book and not listening.

"Just him," explained Dani, and he undid a button. The face and whiskers of a white kitten appeared in the gap for a moment, then pulled back inside.

"Dani," cried Annette, horrified, "you're a very, very naughty boy! You know Grandmother said you couldn't have kittens in the hospital. I don't know what we shall do with him."

Dani gazed thoughtfully out of the window and said nothing. He couldn't think of a single excuse for his wickedness, but under his cloak he gave the white kitten a secret squeeze. The white kitten curled its warm body against Dani's and purred like a little steam engine, and neither of them felt the least bit sorry about it.

25

Getting Better

Dani went straight to bed when they reached the town. He was taken to a large room full of lame children like himself, with a tired-looking nurse in charge. He took one look at them and decided they needed cheering up, so he offered to do kangaroo hops on his bear crutches all down the ward. It was a great success, and within an hour Dani was friends with everybody. The white kitten was given a basket in the kitchen and was allowed in during visiting time.

Annette's arrival was not quite so happy. She was welcomed kindly by Madame Givet, who was young and pretty and jolly, and taken to her room at the top of the house. When she was left alone, she ran across to the window and looked out to see houses and slushy snow in the streets and low grey skies. She gazed out for a moment and then flung herself on the bed and wept bitterly for her home.

Here Madame Givet found her half an hour later when she came up to see what had happened to her. She said nothing but slipped away and returned with baby Claire in her arms, and laid her down on the bed beside Annette. It was the best thing she could have done. Five minutes later Annette was sitting up smiling, with baby Claire chuckling and giggling on her lap, and in another minute Annette was chuckling back.

She was happy and busy at Monsieur Givet's house. In the mornings she helped Madame and looked after the children, in the afternoons she sat with Dani, and in the evenings she did her lessons. The children were not always good with her, and often, to begin with, Madame Givet would have to be sent for to keep the peace. Although she sometimes felt cross and impatient with them, she tried hard to remember what Grandmother had said. Gradually the love of Jesus in her began to make her patient and kind and unselfish, and she found that she could speak gently and keep her temper.

Dani was in the hospital a week before he had his operation. He went off to the operating room feeling quite excited. But when he woke up hours later, he was very upset to find that his bed had been tipped up and there were large iron weights on the end of his leg, which hurt dreadfully. He felt sick and hot, and screamed for Annette.

All that week Dani lay on his back, with the

weights hanging on his leg, feeling feverish and miserable. Annette came every day and read to him and told him stories and tried to make him forget how badly his leg was hurting him. But it was a miserable week. Dull clouds hung low over the grey waters of the lake, and Dani tossed and fretted and tried to be brave but couldn't manage it.

In those long days there was just one thing that comforted Dani. On the wall opposite him was a picture with some writing under it that Dani couldn't read. When he was tired of the pain, and tired of stories, and tired of the grey lake and the other children, he looked at his picture, because he never got tired of it.

It was a picture of the Lord Jesus sitting in a field of flowers, and the children of the world were standing around him, looking up into his face. On the grass at his feet sat a black boy, and on his knee was an Indian child. His arms were around a little girl in a blue dress, and the children of China and the South Seas were nestling up to him.

It was about a week after the operation when Dani and Annette first talked properly about that picture. The lights were on, and most of the children were asleep, but Annette still sat beside Dani. She had stayed late the past few nights because he was so restless without her.

Now he lay with his arms flung around his head on his pillow. His eyes were very bright. He was very, very tired and wanted badly to go to sleep, but the pain in his leg kept him awake. So he rolled his head around to look at the picture with the writing underneath.

"What does it say, 'Nette?" asked Dani suddenly.

"It says, 'Let the little children come to me,'" replied Annette, who was looking tired, too.

"I know that story," went on Dani, in a tired little voice; "Grandmother told it to me. Are those the children in the Bible?"

"No," said Annette, "they're not the children from the Bible story, Dani. They are other children from all over the world—India and Africa, and I think the little girl in the blue dress is probably from Switzerland."

"Why?" asked Dani.

"I suppose to show that all children can come to Jesus, and not just the ones in the Bible."

"How?" asked Dani.

"I don't know quite how to explain. You just say you want to come, Dani, and then you're there. I suppose Jesus sort of picks you up in His arms, like the children in the Bible, even though you can't see Him."

"Oh," said Dani, "I see. Annette, my leg hurts so badly. I wish I could go to sleep."

He began to cry fretfully and throw his arms about. Annette shook up the pillows and gave him a drink, and he sank back with a tired sigh.

"Sing to me," he commanded, and Annette sang very softly because she was shy of the nurse hearing.

As she sang, Dani closed his eyes.

In the few seconds before he fell asleep, Dani thought he saw the picture again, but instead of the Indian child sitting on Jesus's lap, he recognized himself, with his bear crutches lying in the grass at his feet.

"It's me," said Dani to himself, and he fell fast asleep, full of joy.

While Dani lay sleeping, Monsieur Givet came and lifted one of the weights off his leg, and his fever left him. When he woke up he thought he must somehow have gotten into a new world, and he lay quite still thinking about it for a long time. He felt cool and comfortable, and his leg had stopped hurting. The big glass doors of the ward had been flung open, and through them Dani could see, for the first time, sparkling blue water, misty blue mountains on the other side of the lake, and blue sky.

"I'm going to get well," said Dani to himself.

The door opened, and Annette clattered up the ward, warm and rosy from the wind. She usually popped across after breakfast just to see how he was.

"Isn't it a lovely day, Dani?" she cried. "Look at the lake and the mountains on the other side, and the little ships."

Dani turned his face seriously toward her.

"Annette, where are my bear crutches?"

"Here, Dani, behind your locker. Why?"

"Well, you know that poor little boy in the corner? He might like them. Give them to him."

"Why, Dani? You like them so much yourself."

"I know. But I shan't want them ever anymore. I'm going to get better and run about in ordinary boots."

And he was quite right. He never did want them anymore. He became perfectly well.

26

A New Start

Just as the weeks passed in the valley, so the weeks passed in the mountains. The snow began to melt, and the little streams became torrents, and the first crocuses pushed up in the fields along the river. The cattle and goats shut up in the stables began to stamp restlessly and cry for freedom. Spring was coming to the mountains.

Grandmother was busy with the spring cleaning and Papa was busy with the new calves. This was a good thing, for when they were busy they did not miss the children quite so badly. Grandmother, who was really much too old and blind to be spring cleaning, would often sit down suddenly and imagine she heard the hop and clatter of one boot and one crutch climbing the steps, and the cheerful sound of a little boy singing out of tune. How they missed the children!

Lucien missed them, too. He lived farther up the mountain than any other child, and he never walked home alone without wishing Annette was walking beside him. But he was not lonely or unhappy at school any longer. He had proved to them that he was sorry for what he had done by his brave journey across the mountain, and they had accepted him back as one of themselves.

And Lucien himself was different. Ever since that night when he had asked Jesus to come into his heart, he had known that there must be a difference. The old bad temper and laziness and unhappiness could not stay for long in a heart that was open to the love of Jesus. Gradually Lucien began to find that, as long as he kept close to Jesus by praying and reading his Bible every day, the love was stronger than the bad temper and the laziness, and that he was growing into a nicer sort of boy.

Often when school was over he would go across to Grandmother's chalet and help with the spring cleaning. They were great friends now. Indeed, Grandmother would hardly have known what to do without him, for he chopped her wood and did her shopping and brought letters up from the village. This he liked best of all, for they were usually from Annette, and Grandmother always got him to read them aloud to her. There was sometimes a picture from Dani, too. Grandmother kept them all safely in the front of her Bible and often spread them out on the table to look at them. By the end of February she had quite a collection, called "Me in Bed," "Me Chasing Goats," "Me Having Medicine," "Me and Nurse," "Me and Annette," "Me and Snowball-Kitten." Grandmother thought they were all lovely, of course.

Another sadness came into Lucien's life. His friend, the old wood carver, was going to leave the mountain to go and live down by the lake with his son, Monsieur Givet, and his family. It had all been arranged that afternoon when they first recognized each other.

He was to leave at the beginning of March, and the day before he went Lucien climbed up through the forest to help him pack. He had given away the goat, the cat, and the hens, and sold nearly all his little figures. But he was not selling the house. He was just shutting it up to wait till he came back.

"I shall often come back, Lucien," he explained. "I couldn't leave the mountain for long. I'll stop down there for a while, but then I shall hear the mountains calling me, and back I'll come for a bit of a holiday."

He looked thoughtfully across the valley, then glanced around the bare shelves of the hut.

"I'm taking a few of my figures for the children," he remarked. "They may like them. One, Lucien, I kept for you. I came across it when I was sorting through them the other night. It's one I thought I couldn't part with, but I'd like you to have it if you'd like it."

Lucien looked up eagerly. "I'd love to have one, Monsieur," he replied. "It will remind me of you, and besides, I might be able to copy it."

The old man went to the cupboard and took out the gift he had laid aside for Lucien. He put it in the boy's hands and watched him closely as he examined it.

It looked simple enough at first sight. It was a wooden cross made of two pieces of rough wood, but the crossbeam was fixed to the post by beautifully carved ropes, twisted in knots. Lucien's fingers touched the perfect carving gently, and he lifted shining eyes to his old master.

"It's beautiful," he cried. "I can't think how you carved those ropes without breaking the wood." Then he added rather shyly, "It's the cross where Jesus was crucified, isn't it?"

"Yes," replied the old man simply. "I carved it the night my master died—the night he spoke to me about the love and mercy of God—and the night I believed I could be forgiven. Once you and I had a talk about loving. The cross is the place where we see love made perfect."

Lucien looked up again quickly.

"Perfect love," he repeated. "That's what it says in Grandmother's verse. It keeps coming. It's what Annette and I talked about the night before she went away."

"Yes," agreed the old man. "You'll often hear it. Perfect love. It means love that goes on doing until there isn't any more to be done, and that goes on suffering until it can't suffer any more. That's why, when Jesus hung on the cross, He said, 'It is finished.' There wasn't one sin left that couldn't be forgiven, not one sinner who couldn't be saved, because

He had died. He had loved perfectly."

The old man seemed to have forgotten Lucien and to be talking to himself. But Lucien was listening all the same. He said good-bye to his old friend and promised to come up early next morning and carry his pack to the station on the way to school. Then he ran home. He was in a hurry because he wanted to write to Annette so that the old man could take a letter with him next morning. But the first thing to do was to hang his little cross carefully above his bed. Then he ran out to the kitchen to find a pen and paper.

The kitchen was in rather a mess. His mother was over with the cows and had not had time to wash the pans or empty the bucket. Lucien usually helped her, but tonight he was in a hurry. If he slipped back into his bedroom he could write without being disturbed, and she would clear the mess and not know he had come in.

He hurried off and curled himself up on the floor by his bed. He was just starting to write when he happened to glance up and caught sight of the carved cross hanging on the wall.

He stared at it for a moment or two, thinking hard. What was it the old man had said? "Perfect love goes on doing until there isn't anything more to be done."

He in some small way wanted to be like Jesus and to love perfectly, too. And there were all those dirty pans out in the kitchen waiting to be washed.

He went rather pink and got up slowly. When his mother came in half an hour later, she found the kitchen all clean and tidy and a happy-hearted

Lucien writing at the table.

He went up to the old man early next morning while the forest was still dark, and they came down together, leaving the lonely hut waiting for his return.

The old man went off on the train that had carried away Annette and Dani, and his eyes fixed sadly on the mountains.

"When the narcissi begin to come out, I shall come back," he reminded Lucien as the train was starting off. "You write and tell me when they're out in the valley, and that will give me plenty of time to get back before they flower in the mountain. Don't forget, Lucien."

It was not very long after this that Lucien collected a letter for Grandmother from the post office and hurried up the hill to give it to her, for he knew it was from Annette. He clattered up the veranda steps shouting the good news, and Grandmother came eagerly out.

"Read it to me, Lucien," she said, and sat down in the sunshine, folding her hands and shutting her eyes so she could concentrate on the words.

It was a very short letter, and Lucien read it all in one breath.

"Dear Papa and Grandmother," it said, "Dani and I are coming home the day after tomorrow. Dani is quite well again. We are longing to see you, and Dani says please bring Klaus to the station. Your loving Annette."

There was also a note from Madame Givet giving the exact time of their arrival, and a picture from

Dani called, "Me Coming Home in the Train."

Just for a few minutes Grandmother began to cry —the shaky little cry of a very weak old woman— but she quickly wiped away her tears and pretended to become a very strong old woman, because there was such a lot to be done.

"Go over to the shed and give that letter to Monsieur Burnier, Lucien," she said firmly, "and then come back here and help me right away. There's a lot to be done—beds to air, cakes to cook, and the furniture to be rubbed up. We must have everything looking its best for the children."

Papa, on receiving the news, said, "Oh!" and scratched his head. Then for the first time in his life he upset the milk pail, and shortly afterward disappeared into the forest and didn't come back for a long time.

The next day dawned clear and beautiful. There was no school. Lucien was up at daybreak picking flowers. He arranged them in a bowl on the veranda table and then set out for the station, walking slowly because there was plenty of time and plenty to think about. Grandmother, Papa, and Klaus had gone in the mule cart.

It was such a lovely spring morning, not unlike the day just over a year ago when Dani had fallen, thought Lucien. What a dark day that had been. The memory of it spoiled his happy thoughts. It had all been his fault they had ever had to go away, and perhaps after all they wouldn't be very pleased to see him. Annette had said Dani was well, but Lucien could hardly believe it.

He reached the station feeling very nervous, and stood away from the others, with his hands in his pockets, because he suddenly felt a little afraid of meeting them, and wished he hadn't come.

Papa kept his eyes fixed on the far point down the valley where the train would appear between the mountains, and Grandmother struggled with Klaus, who seemed to want to set off down the line and meet the train on her own.

"It's coming," cried Papa.

Lucien suddenly felt shier than ever.

When it came, Annette and Dani were at the window, rosy with excitement and longing to get out.

Dani gave one glance at the well-loved faces that had come to welcome him, and in that glance he noticed Lucien standing apart. For an instant he wondered why. His loving, happy little heart wanted to gather everyone together about him, and he jumped off the train and ran straight to Lucien.

"Look, Lucien," he shouted, "I can walk! The doctor you found made me better, and I can run just as though I never fell over the ravine. Look, Grandmother! Look, Papa! I'm running without my crutches! And look, Klaus, here's your kitten. Isn't he big, Grandmother? Nearly as big as Klaus!"

Klaus and the kitten simply hated each other, and snarled and scratched and swore dreadfully. Dani and Grandmother struggled to keep them apart, everyone laughed, the train rattled off, and Annette clung to her father as though she would never let go of him again.

Only Lucien turned away, because he found there

were tears in his eyes. He had been honored above everybody. The wrong he had done had been forgiven and forgotten forever. Dani could walk as if he had never fallen.

Spring had come. The winter was over and gone. With the flowers appearing and the birds singing again, joy had returned to their hearts.

The Tanglewoods' Secrets

In a struggle to overcome her fiery temper and selfish spirit, Ruth is led to the discovery of a very important Shepherd who can and does teach her (and others) how to be good. The story contains beautiful and uplifting examples of what can happen when we let ourselves be found by Him.

ISBN-10: 0-8024-6576-5   **ISBN-13: 978-0-8024-6576-4**

Star of Light

Set in North Africa, _Star of Light_ is about a little boy's love for his sister, who is blind, and how he rescues her from being sold into an inevitable life of abuse.

ISBN-10: 0-8024-6577-3   **ISBN-13: 978-0-8024-6577-1**

Rainbow Garden

When Elaine leaves her home in London to stay with the Owen family in Wales, she feels miserable and left out. Only the little secret garden that she finds at the end of the rainbow, makes staying there seem worthwhile. And then something happens that changes everything.

ISBN-10: 0-8024-6578-1   **ISBN-13: 978-0-8024-6578-8**

The Secret at Pheasant Cottage

Lucy has lived with her grandparents at Pheasant Cottage since she was a little girl but she has a dim memories of someone else. Who was it? What are her grandparents hiding from her? Lucy is determined to find the answers but it turns out to be harder than she expected.

ISBN-10: 0-8024-6579-X   **ISBN-13: 978-0-8024-6579-5**